nystery

tricate,
full of

oks, 85
me the
nviable

2 9 AUG 2017

- 2 DEC 2017

8/3/18
Barnos

D1610181

Please return on or before the latest date above.
You can renew online at www.kent.gov.uk/libs
or by phone 08458 247 200

CUSTOMER SERVICE EXCELLENCE

Libraries & Archives

deleted

THE ADVENTURES OF PAUL PRY
THE CASE OF THE CARELESS CUPID
THE CASE OF THE FENCED-IN WOMAN
THE CASE OF THE MISCHIEVOUS DOLL
THE CASE OF THE MUSICAL COW
THE CASE OF THE NERVOUS ACCOMPLICE
THE CASE OF THE PERJURED PARROT
THE CASE OF THE PHANTOM FORTUNE
THE CASE OF THE POSTPONED MURDER
THE CASE OF THE RESTLESS REDHEAD
THE CASE OF THE SCREAMING WOMAN
THE CASE OF THE SHOPLIFTER'S SHOE
THE CASE OF THE SMOKING CHIMNEY
THE CASE OF THE SPURIOUS SPINSTER
THE CASE OF THE STEPDAUGHTER'S SECRET
THE CASE OF THE STUTTERING BISHOP
THE CASE OF THE VAGABOND VIRGIN
THE DA BREAKS A SEAL

ERLE STANLEY GARDNER

THE DA
CALLS A TURN

HOUSE OF
STRATUS

This edition published in 2000 by The House of Stratus, an imprint of Stratus Books Ltd., 21 Beeching Park, Kelly Bray, Cornwall, PL17 8QS, UK.

www.houseofstratus.com

Typeset, printed and bound by The House of Stratus.

A catalogue record for this book is available from the British Library and the Library of Congress.

ISBN 1-84232-099-8

CHAPTER ONE

Mrs Freelman opened the oven door, and the aroma of roasting turkey flooded the kitchen. She lifted the lid of the roaster for an expert appraisal of the browning bird, then closed the oven door and nodded to Corliss Ditmer. "In about thirty minutes," she said.

Seen in repose, Corliss Ditmer would definitely never have won any beauty prizes. Her complexion was neither white-skinned nor evenly bronzed. Her short, turned-up nose supported a pair of large-lensed spectacles ... But persons seldom saw Corliss Ditmer in repose.

Overflowing with animation, her good-natured personality welded her physical features into an individuality. No one ever thought of Corliss as a chunky, muddy-complexioned girl with glasses, any more than one would have thought of electricity as a round copper wire.

Corliss was engaged to Edward Freelman. The date of the wedding depended quite frankly on the war and finances, yet neither would accept help from the family. "This marriage," as Edward had explained to his father, "is something very personal – something we're doing on our own."

"Ma" Freelman opened the warming oven in the top of the stove to make certain that the mince pies were being kept at just the right temperature. There were always a thousand and one little things to be done right at the last moment on a Thanksgiving dinner. Corliss was a big help. Somehow, details simply melted off the girl's fingers.

Outside, the sun was brilliant and warm and not too hot, for which Mrs Freelman was profoundly thankful. That section of Southern California in which Madison City was located had a habit of staging some of its hottest weather during the desert-wind month of November. Cooking a Thanksgiving dinner during a spell of desert weather would have changed a culinary joy to a tedious chore.

Ma Freelman, in the middle fifties, with white hair and a florid complexion, always perspired when she hurried, and a quick look in the mirror convinced her that her face would take a dash of cold water and a quick dusting with powder.

Corliss seemed to read her thoughts.

"Go ahead, Ma," she said. "I'll hold things in line. They'll want a cocktail, anyway."

Mrs Freelman smiled gratefully. "Now don't you worry about things, Corliss. Just leave 'em the way they are. I'll be right back."

Corliss nodded, crossed the kitchen with quick springy steps, stiff-armed the swinging door, and called across the dining-room to the family group in the living-room, "How about it? You boys going to have a cocktail?"

It was Stephen, the oldest boy, who answered. "*I'll* say we're going to have a cocktail."

"Ice cubes, cocktail shaker, bottles, and glasses on the sideboard," Corliss said, "and they get whisked off that sideboard five minutes before dinner. That will be exactly twenty minutes from now."

Stephen came into the dining-room and said, "Good girl, Corliss." He didn't need to ask who had been responsible for the efficient arrangement on the sideboard. The Freelman family took Corliss for granted. More and more they let her assume domestic responsibilities in which no stranger would have been permitted to share.

There were no daughters in the family to help Ma Freelman with her dinners. There were the three boys who were home: Stephen, thirty-six; Gilbert, thirty-four; and Edward, twenty-two. There was one vacancy in the family group. Frank Freelman, the fourth brother, was in the Navy on a destroyer, but they had received a letter from him only the week before, saying he was safe, sound and healthy. Bernice, Stephen's wife, was from a wealthy family. She was accustomed to servants, and her household experience was as an executive rather than a worker. She seemed genuinely to enjoy these visits to Stephen's parents, but she definitely didn't fit in the kitchen. She was willing enough, but hopelessly inept. Keeping up with the pace Ma Freelman set in the kitchen was a job for a specialist. No dilettante housewife could have qualified.

Carmen, Gilbert's second wife, was almost a stranger. They had been married only four months. She was years younger than her husband, and this was Carmen's first attendance at a family gathering. Gilbert was a shipyard executive, lately grown grave and thoughtful. Carmen had charge of advertising and personnel for a chain of Los Angeles and suburban grocery stores. The directors considered her so indispensable they had made her promise to stay on for at least six months after her sudden marriage. Her ideas of cookery were very frankly confined to frying and can-opening.

At this Thanksgiving gathering the whole family was trying hard to "be nice to Carmen" and "make her feel at home."

Corliss rebelled at this. She had said earlier to Ma Freelman, "Why don't they quit being so obvious about it and just start treating her as one of the gang? Poor kid, she's feeling as conspicuous as a black eye on a bridegroom ... Oh, well, a cocktail will help out."

And Stephen's cocktail did help out. It was mixed with meticulous care, and with all those little flourishes of exactitude which mark a man who is accustomed to having things just so and, what is more, who knows how to make them just so.

By the time they gathered around the table, everyone was in high good humour.

"Dad" Freelman, at the head of the table, had what Corliss referred to as his "naughty" twinkle in his eyes. A solid, substantial, shrewd rancher, Charles W Freelman had worked hard to get the things he wanted. His citrus ranch produced just a little better oranges and lemons than any of his neighbours. He was inordinately proud of his boys: Stephen, with his real estate business in the city; Gilbert with the responsibility of turning out ships and more ships; Frank who had left a good position to join the Navy; and Edward, the youngest, working in an airplane factory at Burbank, but who was deferring his wedding date because he intended to join the Army, trying to get into the service as part of an airplane ground force in China.

Dad Freelman glanced around the table, pushed back his chair and got to his feet. "Got to stand up," he explained, "to get leverage on this turkey."

"Now, don't make that turkey sound tough," Ma Freelman said, "and don't take off your coat."

"I'd like to know why I'm not going to take off my coat," Dad Freelman said truculently. "I've been carving turkey with my coat off for more than thirty Thanksgivings that I can remember. You can't carve a turkey sitting down, and you can't carve a turkey with your coat on."

Even if Carmen hadn't realized that Mrs Freelman's concern had been for her, the shifting eyes of the others in the family would have made her aware of it. She laughed and said, "I don't think I've ever seen so big a turkey. You have to stand up to get on an even footing with the bird."

They laughed then, the polite laughter which is so different from the spontaneous merriment accorded to a sally from one who has been adopted into the family.

The telephone rang just as Dad Freelman's knife slid smoothly along the juicy white meat.

"I'll get it," Ma Freelman said, pushing back her chair. "Now you folks sit right still. Go ahead. Go ahead and serve, Pa."

"Carmen," she called a moment later, "long distance wants you."

Carmen hurried to the phone. There was a brief period of strained silence; then with a rush everyone started talking at once. There was a great deal of laughter as the steaming plates began to move down the table.

Then Carmen had hung up and was coming back, looking as though someone had slapped her in the face with a freshly emptied flour sack.

Her haunted, tortured eyes caught those of Mrs Freelman. Ma Freelman knew that she must keep the others from looking at Carmen, knew that she must say something quickly to centre attention on herself. Yet, for a long agonizing moment, the words wouldn't come.

It was Corliss who gave the conversational ball a verbal kick, and Carmen sat down amid the quick laughter which followed.

Carmen picked up her fork. Stephen said to Edward, "And you are planning to come back to Madison City to live!"

"There's nothing wrong with Madison City," Ed insisted.

"What there is of it," Gilbert said.

"Bunk," Ed retorted. "You people who go away to the city are driving yourselves nuts with the strain of it. You've joined the throng of fingernail-biters."

Stephen said, "Look at our women, fresh guy. You don't see any evidences of fingernail-biting there, do you?" He reached over and grabbed Carmen's hand to hold it up, showing the long, pointed nails, coloured a vivid crimson. "The nails of sophistication," he proclaimed, "the – My gosh, Carmen, your fingers are cold. You're trembling. You – "

The conversation died. They were all looking at Carmen.

Corliss said easily, "You'd have scared anyone grabbing her wrist like that. Why don't you pick on someone your own size? Grab that!"

Corliss pushed out a clenched fist, and slowly, but with a distinct effort, the party got under way once more.

There was another call for Carmen about three o'clock, and at four she made her announcement. "I'm definitely *not* going to break up the weekend," she said. "Something has gone wrong at the office, and I've got to run in and dig out some papers for the big boss ... I'm taking the car and running in. I'll be back by ten or eleven o'clock."

"But, honey," Gilbert protested, "I'll drive you in. You're not going alone."

"That's just it. I'm not going to interfere with the family party, Gilbert."

"Not the way the tyres are, honey. You let me drive and – "

"Don't be silly! I won't have any blowouts at night. I'll be back here by ten-thirty or eleven at the latest ... He *would* have to go down to the office and start prowling around on Thanksgiving. Why can't the man be civilized?"

Stephen said, "As far as breaking up the Thanksgiving gathering is concerned, I've got to do that myself. I've got to see Jason Gillespie about a real estate deal."

"Not on Thanksgiving, Stephen!" Ma Freelman protested.

Stephen said, "It's his own suggestion. He told me yesterday he wanted me to come up. What do you know about Gillespie, Ed?"

"Nice car. Big house," Ed said. "Retired banker. Comfortably fixed. Been here about three years. Widower. Popular. Luncheon club president."

Gilbert said, "I wish you birds would keep your sordid business affairs out of my domestic life. The point is, whether my wife is going to drive to Los Angeles alone."

Carmen glanced appealingly to Ma Freelman. "*You* make him stay."

Edward laughed. "You're on dangerous ground now. It's a talking point with this family that no one ever made anyone in the family do anything."

"It's time then," Carmen announced firmly, "that there was a change in your ideas of home discipline. *I'll* make you stay."

Corliss came in from the kitchen brandishing a rolling pin. "Here you are, dear," she said. "I've always found right behind the ear was the most satisfactory place."

CHAPTER TWO

Doug Selby, Madison County's Young District Attorney, had spent Thanksgiving evening with Rex Brandon, the grizzled old cattleman who bad been elected sheriff on the same ticket which had cleaned out the "courthouse ring" and swept Selby into office.

There was between these two a friendship which had stood the test of time. They worked together with that frictionless efficiency which made their friends triumphant and their political enemies impotent.

Mrs Brandon, who had shared in her husband's career for more than a quarter of a century, taking the bitter along with the sweet and developing a calm philosophy in the process, had cooked a cosy, intimate dinner which included what she referred to as "all the trimmin's." Moreover, she had done it with effortless ease.

Mrs Brandon had, on occasion, cooked for thresher crews and for cowpunchers, and cooking dinner for only three persons was for her such a simple procedure that she "hadn't turned a hair." She ate what she felt she needed and liked her men to "eat hearty." As a result, some hours after the meal, Selby and the sheriff were now relaxing in a deliciously languorous state of physical and mental well-being while Mrs Brandon had gone up to bed some thirty minutes earlier.

Abruptly the telephone rang.

Brandon got to his feet, pushed his stockinged feet down into the comfortable house slippers which were by his chair, and walked over to the wall telephone just as it rang the second time.

"Hello," he said. "Sheriff Brandon speaking."

Doug Selby, watching the sheriff's back, saw him slouching easily against the wall. Then suddenly his back stiffened. He said, "Wait a minute. What's that name? Oh, Doug, get this, will you? Carleton Grimes, G-r-i-m-e-s … It isn't? Oh, I see. G-r-i-*n*-e-s. You spell it with an *n*. That right? And you say you've stolen a car? Where'd you steal it?

"I see. Over in Las Alidas, eh? Just parked at the kerb, eh? Where are you now? … And you're going to stay there? … – You say your brother's in Oklahoma and you're going to see him … Pervis. P-e-r-v-i-s. Is that right? And he lives at 952 East Payside, P-a-y-s-i-d-e, Street, Cherokee Flats … Well, you just stay right there at the telephone. I'll send somebody down to pick you up."

Sheriff Brandon hung up the telephone, turned to Selby, and grinned. "A drunk with a crying jag. He's sobbing over the telephone about how he's breaking the hearts of his whole family, and has gone out and got crocked again. He's evidently been in trouble before. This time he stole a car over in Las Alidas. He wants to know if the thing can be squared some way. He's on his way to see his brother."

"Where is he?" Selby asked.

"Up in the Orange Heights subdivision."

Selby said, "Why would a drunk steal a car and go up to Orange Heights?"

"Darned if I know."

Brandon called the sheriff's office at the courthouse, said, "Hello, who's on duty? Frank Gordon? Okay. Frank, there's a drunk with a crying jag and a stolen automobile up at Orange Heights – intersection of Orange Grove and Madison Avenue.

He wants to give himself up. It's a car that he picked up in Las Alidas; says his name is Grines from Cherokee Flats, Oklahoma; has a brother there ... Better go pick him up and – When did he go? Wait a minute."

Brandon stood at the telephone thinking for a moment, then said, "Okay, Frank, forget it. I'll go myself and bring him in."

He hung up the telephone, turned to Selby, and said, "The other deputy's out on a call, and Frank Gordon's there all alone ... I'm just a little afraid this drunk may get in that car and start driving."

"How about notifying the city police?" Selby asked.

Brandon grinned. "That intersection is just about fifty feet outside the city limits. Otto Larkin, our dear chief of police, never would get done beefing ... Come on, Doug, take a ride. I'll drop you by your apartment on the way back."

Selby tapped the ashes out of his pipe. "Oh, well," he said, thrusting the hot brier into his pocket, "why not? It'll give this drunk another shoulder to cry on."

Brandon stepped to the hall door by the foot of the stairs, called gently, "You awake, Mother?"

Mrs Brandon called down sleepily, "The phone wakened me. What's the matter?"

"Doug and I are going out on a little call," Brandon said cheerfully. "Should be back pretty quick. Go to sleep, Mother."

"Don't work too late," she said.

Rex Brandon kicked off his slippers, thrust his feet into low boots. "Okay, Doug, let's go."

The night was turning crisp, with frost-polished stars blazing steadily down. Brandon slid in behind the steering wheel of the county car. Selby got in beside him. Brandon kicked on the starting switch, and, at the same time, clicked on the red spotlights which denoted he had a police car travelling on official business. "Reckon we might as well get there and get it over with soon as possible ... If you don't mind, Doug, you could drive that stolen car up to the courthouse, and I'll take the drunk with me."

"Okay," Selby said, opening his tobacco sack and pushing more tobacco into his pipe.

"Funny thing," Sheriff Brandon mused, swinging the big car around a corner. "A fellow gets potted and does a lot of things he really doesn't *want* to do. This chap had evidently been trying to go straight; then he had a couple of shots and took a nose-dive. He straightens out enough to find himself with a strange automobile and a snootful, and darned if he doesn't telephone the sheriff … Something kinda decent about that. Don't you s'pose we could go sorta light on him, Doug?"

"Perhaps," Selby said, then added after a moment, "it'll depend on the circumstances. They may have been too easy with him before. Bet you even money he's on parole or probation right now."

"No dice," Brandon said, throwing the car into second and starting the long grind which led up to Orange Heights. "He said he'd been in trouble before and his brother had got him out."

"Mead's service station is closed," Selby said, looking up toward the top of the grade. "Looks as though there's a car in front of it."

"That's right, a car standing still, but the headlights are on," Brandon said.

The county car rolled up the steep incline for another hundred yards; then Selby said, "I guess I was wrong, Rex. That car really is moving. Coming right along."

A boulevard stop loomed ahead. The sheriff turned on the siren.

"I wouldn't trust the siren to clear the way," Selby warned hastily. "That's the alternate through-highway. Heavy trucks detour the city traffic by using it."

"I'll throw a scare into 'em," Brandon said, his foot swinging for the brake pedal. "But I won't go across unless I see it's clear. I – "

"Here comes one!" Selby exclaimed.

They were close enough to the intersection to see a big truck and trailer grinding down the highway at high speed. Brandon slammed on the brake, muttered, "Those birds are supposed to stop for a siren. They get by with it because if you're really on official business, you're too busy to stop and make a pinch; and if you aren't, you aren't usin' the siren and spotlight."

Brandon twisted one of the red spotlights so it was shining directly on the cab of the truck. "Perhaps that'll slow him down. It – "

"Look!" Selby shouted. "Across the street, Rex, coming this way!"

Selby pointed excitedly to headlights which, sweeping down from Orange Heights, were far over on the left-hand side of the street and approaching the intersection at high speed.

"He'll hit that truck," Brandon shouted. "He – "

The oncoming headlights veered sharply as the car struck the kerb, then swerved. The truck and trailer and the oncoming sedan joined in a crashing vortex of destruction. Lights on both cars went out. Metal screamed as it was wrenched loose. The trailer swung crazily around as though it had been on the end of some gigantic crack-the-whip. A car coming from the east tried to stop, and the screaming of its tyres on the pavement added to the mêlée of sound and confusion; then the side-skidding trailer smashed into it with a crash that punctuated the orgy of wrecking in a final exclamation point of destruction.

The silence which followed on the heels of that last crash seemed absolute; then a woman screamed. Somewhere a child was crying.

Selby was out of the county car, running across to the scene of the wreck. A woman was sprawled flat on the pavement.

Another, on her hands and knees, lurched blindly as she tried to get to her feet, then staggering a few steps, fell flat. The crying of the child became louder. A man lay crumpled, half in and half out of the wrecked sedan which had raced down the Orange Heights grade.

Brandon drove his car out on the highway. His two spotlights blazing directly up and down the road brought all traffic to a stop. A man with an overcoat thrown over pajamas emerged from a near-by lunch counter to say, "I've phoned the sheriff's office. They're sending an ambulance – Well, doggone if it ain't the sheriff. How'd *you* get here?"

Brandon said, "Help get these people up off the highway. Get the kids out of that wrecked car … There's a fire extinguisher in my car. Get it out. We don't want a fire."

"Okay, Sheriff."

Curious spectators came from nowhere to form a ring around the little group. Some, seeing there was work to be done, pitched in and took a hand. Others withdrew just far enough to keep from being called to help, close enough to drink in the spectacle with morbid curiosity.

Selby and the sheriff directed the work of getting people removed from the wreckage. Vaguely, Selby was conscious of a man in a leather coat with blood trickling down one side of his face who seemed to be everywhere at once. He was there directly behind Selby when the district attorney lifted a crying baby from the wreckage of the automobile.

"I'll take her," he said.

Selby surrendered the baby and wormed his way through the half opened door toward a whimpering noise. "It's all right, youngster," Selby said reassuringly and stretched his hands down into the darkness.

A bundle of animate fur popped into his arms, still whimpering.

Selby stepped back, and the man said, "I'll take it."

Selby said, "It's a dog." He held a little black woolly dog that was trembling and whimpering.

Someone produced a flashlight. It showed the interior of the wrecked sedan which had contained the women, showed the confusion which had resulted when a suitcase had been forced open, to vomit its contents over the upended cushions.

There was an unconscious child on the floor, a girl five or six years old. The man in the leather coat lifted her out tenderly.

Brandon backed the county car so as to leave a clear channel through which a single stream of traffic could flow in each direction. Cars crawled by in an endless procession. Back on each side of the pool of traffic congestion, curious motorists kept stopping, parking their cars, and getting out to see what was causing the excitement.

An ambulance came whizzing up from the side street, its siren throbbing. Two motorcycle officers roaring up, side by side, kicked supports under their motorcycles, produced flashlights, and went to work with an air of professional competency.

Brandon said, "I want to talk with whoever was driving that truck."

The ubiquitous man in the leather coat and with the cut face bobbed up instantly at Brandon's elbow. "You're talking to him," he said.

"Why didn't you stop when you heard my siren?"

"I didn't hear it. The transmission in that big bus makes an awful grind."

"You saw my red spotlight, didn't you?"

"Yeah, but it was too late then. You was already stopped, and I was enterin' the intersection."

"Why didn't you see this man coming down the hill?"

"Cripes, I did. That's one reason I didn't stop. He was driving crazy. He must have been good and drunk. Look at where he hit the kerb. Then he bounced off the side of that building. He was coming right toward me. I wanted to get across the intersection and out of his way."

Brandon turned to Selby. "We'll take a look at what's left of the driver of that car. Poor Carleton Grines just couldn't stay put."

CHAPTER THREE

Harry Perkins, the Coroner and Public Administrator had two ambulances which he operated in connection with his business. He was a tall, bony, genial man who regarded life with a whimsical detachment. The duties of his office sat lightly on his erect, bony shoulders. Long experience had taught him to regard those whom he transported in siren screaming haste as bits of baggage which must be delivered at high speed. "They burn up the roads," he was wont to say, "getting into smashups, and I rush 'em to the hospitals."

He grinned at Rex Brandon and Selby, and said, "Dogs are a problem. You can take the people to the hospital, and the doctors operate on 'em; but there ain't no place to take a dog … Look at the little cuss. He knows I picked up the family, and that I know where they are. He's sorta lookin' to me."

Selby regarded the wistful eyes of the little black dog.

Perkins went on, "I'm tryin' to find out what his name is. I've been tryin' him with *Sport* and *Blackie* and *Prince* and *Rover*. How about it? You guys think of any good dog names? He don't answer any I've thought up."

Brandon laughed. "I'm afraid you'll have to get someone else to think up dog names for you, Harry. Doug and I want to see the body of the man who was driving the car that came down the hill."

"Looks like he's the one that's responsible for the whole business," Perkins said. "Guess he never knew what struck him.

I've got him stretched out in there just the way he came in. Doc Trueman says he's dead as a mackerel."

"Let's take a look," Selby said.

Perkins looked down at the dog. "Now, you stay there, Fido. He – *Lookit, boys, his name's Fido!* Cripes, lookit that tail! Well, well, good old Fido!"

Selby grinned down at the dog. Brandon stood impatiently by the door. "Come on, Harry. Quit foolin' with that dog … The car that fellow was driving was stolen, and we've got to find out something about him."

Perkins said, "He stinks like a distillery. I ain't even gone through his pockets yet, just brought him in and stretched him out. I had to rush those other people to the hospital … Guess they're going to live all right. Too bad about that woman. She's got a broken hip. There'll be doctor's and hospital bills. The kids aren't hurt much, mostly scared. Okay, boys, come on."

They walked down a long corridor into a rear room which was cold with the aura of death. A figure stretched on a slab was motionless with that cold dignity which comes with utter finality.

The body was that of a man about forty-two, partially bald. The hair that remained had been permitted to grow so that it could be twisted around the bald spot. Now, in the quiet of that cold room, those little vanities were forgotten. The long strand of hair stretched out on the slab like some attenuated queue attached to the man's head.

The body was dressed in a rough tweed suit, baggy and threadbare in places. Quite apparently, it was a ready-made affair. Selby turned back the coat and saw the label of a haberdashery in Oklahoma City.

"Want to go through his pockets?" Perkins asked. "Got to make an inventory. Might as well do it now."

Selby nodded.

Perkins, working with deft skill, took out a jackknife, a soiled handkerchief, nine dollars in currency, sixty-seven cents in change, a cheap watch, a pack of cigarettes about half full, and an envelope addressed "Carleton Grines, General Delivery, Phoenix, Arizona". The envelope was postmarked "Cherokee Flats, Oklahoma", and was empty.

"Right hip pocket's full of broken glass," Perkins reported, gingerly extracting the neck of a broken flask. "That's where some of the liquor smell is coming from … Well, boys, that's the picture."

"No driving licence?" Selby asked.

"No driving licence, no cards, no keys … Strange thing about bums. Don't ever have any keys. Somehow, you can talk about a man not having a home, and it don't mean so much; but when you go through his pockets and don't find a single key, it gives you an empty sort of feeling."

Brandon nodded. "Well," he said, "I guess we'll ring up the police at Las Alidas and tell 'em about the car, and you'd better notify this man's brother, Harry. The name is Pervis Grines, 952 East Payside Street, Cherokee Flats, Oklahoma."

Perkins looked at him in surprise. "How'd you know that?"

Brandon said wearily, "If we'd been sixty seconds earlier, there wouldn't have been any accident. This man telephoned us to come and get him."

"Well, what do you know about that," Perkins said.

For several moments they stood looking down at the body. "Doesn't seem to be smashed up much," Brandon said.

"That's the way with these drunks," Perkins observed. "They tear along at seventy miles an hour, knock down a couple of lamp posts, skid into a lane of traffic, kill four or five people, and about all they have is a headache – which would have come from the booze anyhow. This man wasn't as lucky as most of 'em. He got killed."

Brandon said, "He told me over the telephone he was on his way to see his brother. It was Thanksgiving, and he'd apparently decided to have a few drinks."

"Doesn't look as though he had much to be thankful for," Perkins observed, looking down at the baggy, worn clothes.

Selby said, "That suit's rather small for him."

"Sleeves and pants seem to be about the right length," Brandon said. "The coat's awfully tight across the chest and shoulders."

"I doubt if he could have buttoned it," Selby said. "Let's see if we can. Straighten the coat out. Pull it down ... Look. Those pants don't meet at the top in the waistband by a good two inches. The belt's holding them together."

"And the belt's in the last notch," Perkins said. "Oh, well, that's the way with bums. They pick up a cast-off suit of clothes somewhere. This is probably one that somebody gave him ... Well, I guess there's nothing else we can do, boys. I've got the stuff from his pockets. You've seen it all now."

The others started toward the door, but Selby continued to stand by the body, staring thoughtfully down at it.

"What's the matter, Doug?" Brandon asked, turning back after he had taken a few steps.

Selby said, "The body of an unknown man always fascinates me. I want to know more about him. Take this chap, for instance. He evidently is a periodic drinker. He must have been fairly prosperous at one time. His features indicate considerable force of character. Then he started drinking again. He was going to see his brother. If his visit had been welcome, he'd have planned to arrive for Thanksgiving. As it was, however, he waited until Thanksgiving to start. There's a whole story there ... And then he got drunk, became filled with remorse, and now this ... Poor chap! And there's something incongruous about the body itself – just take a look at those hands, Rex."

"What's the matter with his hands?" Perkins wanted to know.

Selby said, "Look at the nails."

The others came back to look down at the death-discoloured hand. The nails glistened with a waxen sheen. Selby said, "That's a professional job of manicuring."

Perkins scratched the thin hair around his temples. "Doggone," he observed, "can you beat that? A bum with a dilapidated old suit of clothes, and yet he spends dough to have his hands manicured."

"And notice the way his hair's cut," Selby went on. "A bum doesn't ordinarily take that much pride in his personal appearance. He's been combing that hair around over his bald spot … Let me take a look at that envelope again, Harry. I want another look at that postmark."

Perkins passed over the envelope, reading the postmark as he did so. "Cherokee Flats, November 5th, 1941."

Selby held it to the light, studied it carefully, said, "I'm not so sure that's a four, Harry." He turned the envelope over, then said excitedly, "Look, here's the Phoenix stamp. It's very legible. It's 1931."

Perkins said, "I'll be doggoned."

Abruptly Brandon laughed. "I'll tell you what it is. This is an old suit someone hasn't worn for a long time. This letter happened to be in the pocket, and – No, wait a minute. The envelope's addressed to him, but it certainly doesn't look to be any ten years old.

"Now, how would you explain that, Doug?" Brandon asked.

Selby said, "Just making a wild guess, the man might not have seen his brother for ten years. Probably this envelope had contained the last letter he'd ever had from his brother. Oh, well, that's all conjecture. Let's stick to logic."

Brandon glanced at the coroner. "Strikes me Doug's doing all right," he said.

Perkins nodded.

"He was probably carryin' this letter with him," Brandon went on. "He might have had it out, readin' it while he was waitin' out there on the hill. Perhaps it blew out of his hand as he started down that grade."

Selby said, "We're going to get at the bottom of this. There's something strange here. Take a look at those socks. Those socks certainly don't go with the suit."

"They don't for a fact," Perkins said. "Those are expensive, pure-silk socks. I'll bet they're full of holes, though."

Selby unlaced the right shoe, slipped it off. "No holes there … And observe this shoe, Rex. That's an expensive shoe. Notice that the heel isn't the least bit run down. Let's see if the name of the dealer is in the shoe."

He turned the shoe so that the light shone down on the inside. The leather insole was stamped "Bixby Handmade Shoe Company, Los Angeles, California," and it was followed by a number "X03A1."

Perkins indicated the number. "That's the size. They put those things in code so when a person should have a size larger shoe, he doesn't keep trying to crowd his foot into the same old size. This way, a shoe clerk can sell a customer an oversize shoe without the customer knowing anything about it."

Brandon said, "I don't know, Doug. Maybe we've got to the point where we make too much of a mystery out of things. Ordinarily, we'd never even have seen this corpse."

"It's strange, all right," Perkins said breezily, "but you run onto lots of strange things, picking people out of automobile wrecks. If you ask me, this guy managed to promote himself a good pair of shoes and socks, but wasn't so lucky when it came to the suit."

Selby pinched the left shoe, testing the fit with thumb and forefinger. "It's a perfect fit," he announced. "Looks as though it really had been made for him … Tell you what we're going to do. We're going to call Los Angeles, try and get someone who's connected with the Bixby Shoe Company on the line, and see if we can't find out about these shoes. Ordinarily, that number would be a size number, but there's a chance that this relates to a customer's account."

"You won't find anybody this time of night," Perkins said.

"Well, I can try. The Bixby who runs the factory should be listed in the phone book."

They went back to Perkins' office. Selby thumbed through the pages of the telephone book, said, "Here it is, George R Bixby, handmade shoes, a residence address, and also the Bixby Handmade Shoe Company."

Perkins said, "He'll probably cuss you for being pulled out of bed over some bum's shoes."

Selby smiled, said, "Personally, I can't sleep until I find out how those shoes happened to be on such a shabbily dressed individual, and *he* may as well lose a few minutes' sleep as to have me lose a night's sleep."

The call went through almost at once. Bixby evidently had not retired, for his voice sounded crisp and wide awake over the telephone.

"This is the district attorney at Madison City," Selby said. "We're trying to identify a pair of shoes which were made by you. There's a number in them … Yes, I can give it to you. Just a minute."

Perkins handed Selby the shoe, and Selby read the number over the telephone. Bixby said, "Just a minute. I've got a duplicate code book of customers' addresses and sizes here in the house. Just hold the phone a second."

Ten seconds later he said, "That number is one of my good accounts. I thought it was, when you mentioned it, but I wanted to make sure. It's Desmond L Billmeyer, head of the Billmeyer Chain Groceries."

"You have his address?" Selby asked.

"Yes. 9634 Dorton Boulevard, Hollywood."

"Thank you," Selby said, and hung up.

"Well," he told Perkins, "I don't know as it helps any. But the shoes were made for one of his best customers, Desmond Billmeyer of the Billmeyer grocery chain ... Now then, how do you suppose this man got hold of Billmeyer's shoes and how does it happen they fit him so well?"

There was silence for a moment, then Perkins said, "Tell you how you can find out anything you want about Billmeyer. You boys know Gilbert Freelman?"

Selby and the sheriff nodded.

"Well, he married the woman who's Billmeyer's right hand. I saw Charlie Freelman on the street yesterday, and he told me the boys and their wives were going to be there for Thanksgiving."

Selby looked at Brandon. Brandon looked at his watch, then nodded. "Okay, Doug," he said, "let's clean it up."

Chapter Four

It was almost midnight when Carmen Freelman turned her headlights up the driveway to the citrus ranch. The big two-and-a-half-storey structure was still brilliantly lighted. The spacious yard held half a dozen automobiles parked here and there in advantageous places.

Carmen parked the car, ran up the wide, sloping stairs to the veranda. The front door opened and Gilbert switched on the porch light. "I thought I heard a car in the driveway. I was worried about you."

"You shouldn't have waited up," she said. "What was there to worry about?"

In the hallway he held her to him, eagerly, hungrily, as though afraid she might slip from his grasp even while he was holding her. "Hon, it's all right?"

"Why of course it's all right."

"What did he want?"

"Oh, just the usual thing. Mr Big, wanting everybody to know that he was working on Thanksgiving, couldn't find a letter anywhere in the files, and – "

"And it was there?"

"Of *course* it was there! It took me thirty seconds to pull it out and slam it on his desk."

"Then what?"

"Oh, then, since I was there – Let's not talk about it. I'm tired of the whole business atmosphere. Come on, let's go and join the others."

"They're all getting ready for shut-eyes," Gilbert said.

Stephen called from the living-room, "Don't let him kid you, Carmen. Bernice and I were just talking about putting a dance record on the phonograph, taking up the rugs and making whoopee … I just got in a few minutes ago myself."

Carmen moved on into the living-room, her husband's arm around her. "All this time on a real estate deal?" she asked.

"Oh, no," Stephen said. "I got away from Gillespie around seven o'clock, but he raised some questions about the property and I had to run out to take a look. Darned if he didn't have me bothered for a minute, but it's all right. I'll close the deal tomorrow … As far as we're concerned, it's just the beginning of the evening."

Gilbert said, "Carmen won't feel like dancing after driving to Los Angeles and back. How about a drink?"

Carmen glanced over to where Mother Freelman was very frankly fighting off drowsiness. "I don't want your mother to think I'm a fallen woman," she laughed, "but a double Scotch and soda would virtually change my entire outlook on life."

Bernice waved a half-filled glass. "She's dissipating herself. She actually had a ginger ale half an hour ago. Right the way it came out of the bottle!"

Ma Freelman smiled and said, "And it's gone right to my head. You youngsters go ahead and do what you want to. *I'm* going to bed. How about you, Pa?"

Her husband surveyed the assemblage with twinkling eyes. "Haven't finished this cigar yet."

"Pshaw," his wife remarked. "That's just an excuse. You want to sit up and make whoopee with the youngsters. Well, you go ahead. I'm – "

The doorbell rang.

A cloak of quick silence smothered all conversation. They exchanged glances. Mrs Freelman said, "Well, land sakes, we're usually in bed two-three hours before this. I wonder who could be calling this time of night."

"Probably someone wanting to ask about a house number," Carmen volunteered.

Edward burst out laughing. "Go on, fingernail-biter," he said. "Can't you realize you're not in the slums now? You're out where people have elbow room now. This house sits back a quarter of a mile from the road, and the numbers are on the mailboxes, not the houses."

Dad Freelman got up and went out to the entrance hall. They heard him opening the front door, heard him say, "Why, hello, Sheriff. Hello, Selby."

Then Brandon's drawling voice, "Wouldn't have bothered you, Freelman, but we saw the place all lit up."

Edward laughed boisterously. "Well, well," he said, "we're pinched! That's the sheriff and the district attorney."

Corliss laughed. "Now some of you city-dwellers make a crack about *our* party disturbing the neighbours."

With a sudden hectic rush, the conversation became general, an exchange of good-natured, swift banter which reduced the low-voiced conversation in the hallway to a mere rumble.

Dad Freelman's voice rose above their laughter. "Carmen," he called, "would you mind stepping this way? The sheriff wants to see you."

Stephen said jokingly, "That's what you get for running over a pedestrian on a crosswalk, Carmen. You can't square it with a few tears – not in *this* county."

Corliss Ditmer said, "Particularly when you have liquor on your breath and – " She caught the expression on Carmen's face, and stopped abruptly.

Carmen stood straight and white and silent, one hand on the back of her husband's chair; then she said in a voice which sounded thin as a white thread, "Please stay where you are, Gilbert. I'll see what they want."

Gilbert started to rise, then settled back in his chair. There was something almost defiant in the way he tried to make it seem entirely a casual matter, as though challenging the others to look at it in any other light. "Well," he said, "if we're going to turn on some dance music, we'd better take up the rugs."

No one made any move to take up the rugs. Gilbert himself sat very still, trying not to seem to be listening to the low-voiced conversation which was taking place in the corridor.

Abruptly Carmen was in the doorway, smiling at them. "The sheriff wants me to see if I can identify someone. They're going to take me in the county car. I won't be over ten or fifteen minutes."

Corliss said, "Wouldn't you like to have me run along, just to keep you company?"

Gilbert was up out of his chair. His face was very set. "I'm going with you, hon. We'll take our car."

"Don't be silly. It's just a routine something that – "

"No. You've had enough strain for one day."

Gilbert walked out into the hallway. "Why don't you folks come in and have a drink?" he invited. "What's the trouble?"

This time no one made any pretence of not trying to listen. They sat tense, awaiting the sheriff's reply, and it seemed unduly long before he drawled, "We're tryin' to identify a man who may have broken into someone's house. There's just a chance your wife may have seen him somewhere."

Stephen said, "Better watch her, Sheriff. She's got a gun."

They all laughed at that – the overdone laughter which masks anxiety. Then shuffling steps crossed the porch, and purring automobiles slipped smoothly down the driveway and into the night.

Brandon said, "This may be somethin' of a shock, Mrs Freelman. I hate to take you in here, but I don't know just how to avoid it."

Harry Perkins said, "Sit down, Fido. Down."

The black dog promptly sat down. "Gosh, that's a smart dog," Perkins said. "He's got so he minds everything I tell him."

"This is Mr Perkins, Mrs Freelman," Brandon said by way of introduction.

Perkins turned from the dog to say, "How do you do? I'm pleased to know you. I've known your husband ever since he was on the high school debating team. I was one of the judges. Hello, Gilbert. How are you?"

Gilbert shook hands. "What's this all about?" he asked.

Selby said, "Come on, folks. It's like a cold shower. It's disagreeable, but we've got to get it over with … If you don't mind, Mrs Freelman, we'll walk down this passageway."

"Look here," Gilbert protested as they moved down the long corridor, "is this a – "

As he hesitated, Selby said, "Yes, it's a corpse."

"I don't like to have Carmen – "

"Oh, don't be that way," Carmen said. "I've seen corpses before … What makes you think I know him, Sheriff?"

Brandon said, "We want you to look at his shoes, that's all … Now, if you'll just remember this is going to be disagreeable, Mrs Freelman …"

Perkins pulled back a sheet.

For a moment there was utter silence; then Gilbert Freelman exclaimed with a gasp in his voice, "Good heavens! It's Desmond Billmeyer!"

"You're certain?" Brandon asked.

"Why, yes. Carmen works for him." He turned to his wife, slipped his arm around her. "It's a shock, but – it's Billmeyer all right, isn't it?"

She opened her lips and tried to speak. Her trembling lips refused to form words. She glanced appealingly at her husband.

"Hon," he said, "it's all right. It – "

Her knees buckled, letting her drop through his supporting arm, straight to the floor. He didn't catch her until her shoulders had dropped down even with his waist.

"Get her feet, someone," Gilbert Freelman said savagely, "and get her out of here. She had no business coming in here in the first place."

Carmen Freelman, stretched on a couch in the coroner's office and robbed of her animation, seemed thin and weak. Her skin was drained of colour so that the make-up, no longer blending with her complexion, became a garish travesty on nature.

Gilbert said angrily, "You had no right to subject her to a shock of this kind."

Brandon, very dignified now, said, "It's important to get this man identified. It may be *real* important."

"I don't give two hoots in a thunderstorm how important it is. And don't think you're going to question her when she comes out of this. She's had enough for one day."

Brandon said, "But it is Billmeyer all right?"

"Of *course* it's Billmeyer. I've seen him dozens of times."

"When did you see him last?"

"About a week ago."

"When did your wife see him last?"

"She went in to the Hollywood office this afternoon. Billmeyer thought she'd lost a letter. He telephoned her to come in. It was just a grandstand – wanting everyone in the organization to know he'd been working on Thanksgiving."

"Did your wife find the missing letter?" Selby asked.

"It wasn't missing. Making her drive all the way into Hollywood just to pull a letter out of a filing case! Made him feel important!"

"Evidently," Selby said, "you didn't like him."

"I don't – didn't. He's too imbued with the idea of being a big shot."

Carmen stirred slightly. A faint, tremulous sigh came from her lips. Her eyelids fluttered.

Gilbert Freelman turned to face the sheriff. "You understand," he said, "she's not to be questioned. She's gone through enough."

Brandon hesitated. "Well now, Gilbert – "

"I mean that," Gilbert Freelman insisted angrily. "You have no idea of the strain she's been under. She's been anxious to make a good impression upon my family, but that whole set-up is strange to her. Today would have been enough of an ordeal without Billmeyer making her drive to the office so he could keep up his reputation for being an indefatigable worker. And then – "

"Gilbert," Carmen called in a weak, quavering voice.

"Right here, hon."

"Oh … Oh … How did it happen?"

"An automobile accident."

"Where?"

"You mustn't talk about it, hon. Come on, we're going home – if you feel that you can make it."

Selby said, "Look here, Freelman, if we don't ask any more questions tonight, will you promise that Mrs Freelman will be available tomorrow morning?"

Gilbert hesitated.

Carmen said, "Oh, *please* don't let's talk about anything any more. I just want to close my eyes and shut out the recollection of – of – of everything."

Gilbert slid his arm under her shoulders. "Come on, hon. If you feel well enough to walk, we're going to the car."

Selby said, "Here, you can't support her that way. Let me take her other arm."

"No questions," Freelman warned.

Selby smiled. "No questions," he agreed.

Between them, they assisted Carmen down the steps, across the sidewalk, and over to Gilbert's parked automobile.

They opened the car door. Carmen gave Selby a wan smile. "Don't think I'm an awful cry baby," she said, "but I've had – just about all I can stand for one day."

Selby raised his hat. "Ten o'clock in the morning at my office," he said to Gilbert.

Gilbert nodded tersely, slid in behind the steering wheel, and started the car.

CHAPTER FIVE

It was shortly after midnight when Selby entered his office at the courthouse. After the freshness of the night air, the room seemed musty and stale. The leather-backed law books stacked in bookcases from floor to ceiling exuded an atmosphere of ghostly learning. These were compilations of cases in which the litigants were, for the most part, dead and gone – the records of their lawsuits preserved for posterity only because they established legal precedents.

As soon as Selby clicked on the light switch, the office seemed friendly and cheery once more. The skeletons of bygone litigants were pushed back behind the leather bindings of the stacked law books.

Selby crossed over to the telephone and called *The Clarion*.

"Sylvia there?" he asked.

"Just a minute."

While Selby waited, he could hear the clacking of typewriters and the smooth whirr of a linotype machine. Sylvia Martin's cheery, "Hello, Doug," came over the wire. "What are you doing? Playing night-owl?"

"Gone to press yet?" Selby asked.

"We're going in about thirty minutes."

"Hold it," Selby said, "and come up here."

"Can you tell me over the telephone?"

Selby hesitated, said, "I can tell you the part you can publish, but you'll want to know the part you can't publish in order to know the angles on the part I'm ready to release."

She laughed and said, "Sounds Irish. Where are you?"

"At the office."

"Hold everything. I'm coming up."

"I'll go down and unlock the front door for you."

"No need. I've promoted a key. Sold the supervisors on the idea that I had to get in to see officers after hours ... Be seeing you, Doug."

Selby dropped the receiver into place, pushed tobacco down into the bowl of his pipe, struck a match, and puffed thoughtfully at the brier, feeling the glow of companionship in the tobacco as the bowl grew warm in his hand.

In less than five minutes he heard Sylvia's heels in the echoing corridor. He opened the door and she came in, a bundle of quick energy. " 'Lo, Doug. What's the excitement?"

She dropped into a chair, spread folded newsprint over her knee, held a 6B pencil poised, and waited expectantly.

Selby looked her over with evident approval. Her brown eyes, the same shade as her hair and usually filled with smile twinkles, were steady now with concentration. The delicate oval of her face was without expression, making her seem as impersonally efficient as a linotype keyboard.

"Don't look at me like that," she said. "Tell me."

"Was I looking at you like that?" Selby asked.

"I thought so."

"It's a good idea."

"Stop it!" she commanded. "I'm holding the presses up. What's the story? Give it to me fast."

Selby said, "I spent the day at Brandon's place. Around ten-thirty the phone rang. A man who admitted he was intoxicated told Brandon he was Carleton Grines of Cherokee Flats, Oklahoma; that he had a brother named Pervis living at 952 East

33

ERLE STANLEY GARDNER

Payside Street, and was on his way to visit him; that he'd been in trouble before, had promised his brother he'd quit drinking; that he'd fallen off the water wagon, stolen a car in Las Alidas, and was overcome with remorse. He seemed to be in that stage of lachrymose repentance which is popularly known as a crying jag."

"A novel angle there," Sylvia Martin said, making shorthand notes on the newsprint.

"The sheriff and I went out to pick him up," Selby went on. "The place he'd designated was up at the top of the grade which runs down to the main boulevard. Just as we approached we saw a car start down the hill, gathering momentum fast. It swerved crazily, hit the left-hand kerb, and ran into a truck and trailer, swung the trailer around, and hit an oncoming car. It – "

"We have the story of the accident," she interrupted. "Just another car crash. Who owned the stolen car?"

"The registration certificate says Robert C Hinkle of Cherokee Flats, Oklahoma. There's a temporary California certificate with an address in Las Alidas. The sheriff doesn't know anyone by that name over there. Neither do I. We're leaving in a few minutes to check up on that angle ... Remind me to tell you a swell human-interest angle about a dog," Selby said.

"When?"

"For Saturday's paper."

"Why not now?"

"Because I've got a more important angle."

"Shoot."

"The man who was at the wheel of the stolen car was dead. The body was taken to the coroner's office. It was dressed in a rather cheap, ill-fitting suit of tweeds. The coat didn't fit. A lot of things didn't look right. We started an independent investigation. From a label in the shoes we found out they had been made for Desmond Billmeyer – the chain grocery magnate. Perkins thought Carmen Freelman, the wife of Gilbert Freelman, might know something about it. She works for Billmeyer. We went out and got her. She took one look at the body and collapsed in a faint."

"Who was it?" she asked.

"Desmond Billmeyer himself."

"Doug! You're certain?"

He nodded. "Gilbert Freelman also identified him."

Sylvia Martin reached for the telephone, put through a call to the paper, said, "It's a peach of a story. Hold everything. I'll get the details and be down."

She dropped the receiver into place and said, "Give me the details, Doug."

"I've given them to you."

She shook her head. "Those are the things we can publish. Now I want the things we can't publish, and I want them fast."

Selby said, "For the present, this is just between us."

She nodded.

"I'm not entirely certain the man was drunk. I'm not certain he died as a result of the automobile accident."

"What did cause his death?"

"I don't know."

She frowned and said, "But he was dead. He – Doug, you don't mean – "

"Exactly," Selby said. "I mean he may have been dead when that car started down from the top of the hill. The car was stolen. Billmeyer would hardly have stolen it. There was a broken flask in his hip pocket that might have been broken before the car started down the hill … I'm just thinking out loud now, Sylvia."

"Go on, think some more."

"Obviously," Selby said, "*we* wouldn't have known whether Carleton Grines was talking with us or not. A man telephoned and *said* he was Carleton Grines. He seemed intoxicated. He said he'd stolen a car, and for us to send out and pick him up. We were using the siren and the red spotlights. Anyone at the top of the grade could have seen the sheriff's car coming for half a dozen blocks before it got to the through boulevard.

"Some person could have been standing on the running board of the stolen sedan. When the county car came into view, he only needed to take off the emergency brake and turn the automobile loose. It would pick up speed coming down the grade."

"That person couldn't have foreseen the accident at the intersection," Sylvia pointed out.

"No, but an accident at the boulevard was a possibility. The car was almost certain to have crashed into something before it stopped. There's a bump in the road just before you come to the boulevard. A car would have gathered terrific speed by the time it got to that bump. It would have hit *something*."

She tilted back her head and half closed her eyes. "Doug, are you trying to say that someone went to all that trouble to keep you from finding out who Billmeyer was?"

"No."

"What was the reason?" she asked.

"To keep us from finding out how this man died and *when* he died."

"I'm not certain that I get you."

"Nine hundred and ninety-nine times out of a thousand the person driving the sheriff's car, after having seen the crash, would have gone over to the wreckage, found the man dead, and noticed that the odour of whisky was all over the car. He'd have called the coroner's office and washed his hands of the whole business. There'd have been a perfunctory autopsy – probably considerably later on. The sheriff's testimony would have fixed both the cause of death and the time of death – and nothing would have been thought of it. By the time an autopsy was performed, both the clues and the corpse would have been very, very cold. It would then have been a difficult job to tell exactly when the man died."

"But why would anyone want to change the time of his death?"

"I don't know. I'm going to find out. It may be because of an alibi. That's the part you can't publish."

"Doug, you mean he was – *murdered*?"

"I don't know. I have that angle in mind."

"Who knows about this?"

"You do."

"Anyone else? The Los Angeles papers?"

Selby shook his head. "We aren't going to say much until Dr Trueman completes a post-mortem."

"When's that?"

"I got him out of bed. He should be starting on it right now."

Sylvia Martin pushed the folded newsprint into her purse, got to her feet, said, "Okay, Doug, I'm on my way … What was the first tip-off? What made Harry Perkins think he wasn't a bum and look for a label in his shoes?"

Selby said vaguely, "Oh, just two or three little things that didn't fit in."

She said, "Don't be so darn modest. If you won't tell me, I'll get Sheriff Brandon, and *he'll* tell."

Selby said, "Well, I noticed his socks. They were of a quality that didn't go with his tweeds. I noticed his fingernails. They looked manicured. He wore expensive, made-to-order shoes. His clothes were threadbare and too small. An envelope in his pocket had a postmark of ten years ago."

"And if it hadn't been for you," she said, "nothing would have been done until it was too late to run down the clues."

"I wouldn't say that," Selby said.

"*I* would," she told him, smiling. "I'd even put it in writing."

She started for the door, then paused with her hand on the knob. "Why did Carmen Freelman fall over in a faint? Anything particularly gruesome about the remains?"

"That's one of the things you're not publishing – not yet, at any rate."

"Why not?"

"The incident," Selby said, "might be magnified and distorted. With just a little clever innuendo, it could be made to appear their relationship was a little more intimate than would ordinarily have been expected. She's only been married for four months. It will be better if the Los Angeles papers don't know about that."

"You mean they won't find out if I don't tell them," she said, laughing.

"Exactly," Selby told her.

She turned once more toward the door. "You're a good egg, Doug, and too darned considerate for your own good."

CHAPTER SIX

Billy Ransome, the City Marshal and ex-officio chief of police of Las Alidas, a big, good-natured man, came out to meet the sheriff's car.

"Got your telephone call," he said in a low voice. "Let's not talk here. The Little Woman's asleep. I didn't let her know I was going out. She thinks I'm going to get killed every time there's a night call. We can – "

From behind the screen of an open window came a woman's high-pitched rapid voice. "You go ahead and talk right there on the porch, and don't think you're slipping anything over on me, Billy Ransome ... Is that you, Sheriff?"

Brandon, grinning, said good-naturedly, "It's all right, Mrs Ransome, just checking up on a stolen car."

"Well, keep your eye on Billy," she said. "It would be just like him to walk right into a bullet. He's too big to miss."

Brandon nudged Ransome and said, "We may as well talk here. A chap from Oklahoma got drunk and stole a car that's registered as being owned by Robert S Hinkle, 605 Chestnut Street. The car was smashed up and a Los Angeles businessman was killed ... Thought we'd better check up on it. The car has Oklahoma plates. The Las Alidas address is temporary."

"Is that all?" the woman's voice asked.

"That's just about it," Brandon assured her.

They heard the sound of creaking bedsprings. Mrs Ransome said, "All right, Billy, go ahead. And don't you try sneaking out on me again. You hear me?"

"Yes, dear."

"If I'd woke up and found you weren't in the house, I'd have been worse worried than if I'd known you were out chasing a murderer. Now you get started, because I won't go to sleep until you get back."

"Yes, dear."

They walked out to the sheriff's car. Selby said in a low voice, "There's a peculiar angle on the case, Ransome. What do you know about Hinkle? Anything?"

"Not a darn thing," Ransome said. "Want to run around to his address?"

"I think we'd better."

They climbed into the county car. The slamming of doors sounded explosively loud in the quiet neighbourhood. Ransome, looking at the illuminated dial on the dashboard clock, said, "It's ten minutes to two – ain't much of any place for him to be except home. Let's go … Take that first turn to your right, Sheriff, and run down five blocks. That'll put you in the five hundred block on Chestnut. Turn left for a block, and his house will be the second one on the left. We can size it up."

The house was a small California bungalow with a driveway leading to a garage. The house was dark and silent. The deserted sidewalks showed as vague ribbons reflecting the light of the street lamps. The houses themselves loomed with the ghostly silence of tombstones in a graveyard.

Brandon knocked on the door of Hinkle's house. When there was no answer, he knocked again. Selby took a fountain-pen flashlight from his pocket and the beam disclosed a doorbell.

Billy Ransome pressed his thumb against the bell. Brandon continued to knock. After a few minutes a man's sleepy voice called, "Hey, Bob, there's someone at the door."

A light switched on. They could hear the sound of shuffling feet; then the voice said again, "Oh, Bob, somebody at the door."

Brandon called out, "This is the sheriff. We want to talk with you."

More lights came on in the house. After a few minutes a tousle-headed man with sleep-swollen eyes, belting work pants around his middle, opened the front door and looked out through the hooked screen. He switched on the porch lights and said, "What do you guys want?"

"We're looking for Mr Hinkle."

"I'm Hinkle."

Billy Ransome said, "I'm the chief of police here. This is the sheriff and the district attorney."

"Well, what do you want?"

"You own an automobile?"

"Yes."

"Where is it?"

"In the garage. What's the matter?"

"Your automobile has been in a smash-up," Selby said.

"Couldn't have been," Hinkle announced positively.

A woman's voice from the back of the house said, "*Our* car's in the garage, Bob. You left yours in the driveway."

Hinkle rubbed his eyes, scratched around the back of his head, ran his hand through his hair, said dazedly, "Yes, that's right."

There were more feet in the corridor. A rather attractive young woman in a peach-coloured housecoat came to stand in the doorway. She seemed more alert, less sleep-drugged. "What," she asked, "is the matter?"

Selby said, "You say Mr Hinkle's car was in the driveway?"

"Yes. It's right there." She pointed toward the driveway.

Brandon said, "There's no car there now."

"The devil there ain't," Hinkle said.

There were more steps in the corridor, and a man of about thirty-two, in bare feet, wearing pants and shirt, joined the group and surveyed the visitors in sullen-eyed silence. Hinkle unhooked the screen door, walked out on the porch to stare at the vacant driveway.

"You left your car in the driveway?" Selby asked.

Hinkle seemed more wide awake now. "Yes. My friends are visiting me. I put their car in the garage."

"Let's take a look," Selby said.

They walked out to the garage. Hinkle opened the door. A sedan with Oklahoma licence plates was in the garage.

Selby turned to the woman and asked, "What's your name?"

"Grines."

"Of Cherokee Flats, Oklahoma?"

"Yes. How did you know?"

"This your husband? And is his name Pervis?"

The man said, "Yes. What you want?"

Selby asked, "You got a brother by the name of Carleton?"

The man hesitated perceptibly. The woman said, "Of course he has, or did have. He's been dead for ten years."

Selby said, "Someone driving Hinkle's car gave that name."

Pervis Grines said, "Carl was killed in – in Oregon."

"In a jail break in Oregon," the woman supplemented. "That was ten years ago in December, wasn't it?"

"January, 1932," her husband said.

"What's your present residence address in Oklahoma?"

"952 East Payside Street. We own the place. Been there ever since we were married."

"What time did you people go to bed?"

They glanced at each other. "Must have been right around nine o'clock," Hinkle said.

"Isn't that pretty early for Thanksgiving night?"

"I don't know what difference it makes," Hinkle said truculently. "It's a free country. I guess we can still go to bed when we want to, can't we?"

The woman interposed, "Don't be like that, Bob. The man's only trying to find out about your automobile." She turned to the sheriff. "Bob Hinkle works in the oil fields. My husband worked with him in Oklahoma. We had a two-week lay-off and came out to California to look around. We got here Wednesday. Bob's living alone – divorced. I told the boys I'd cook the Thanksgiving dinner. Bob's working. He has to be at work by eight o'clock in the morning, so he went to bed early.

"We know some people a couple of blocks down the street. We went down and had a drink about eight o'clock. Bob didn't go. He thinks they sided with his wife, may have got her to leave him."

"I was tired," Hinkle said sullenly.

"What time did you get back?" Selby asked Mrs Grines.

"About nine-thirty. We looked in on Bob. He was asleep so we didn't disturb him. These people had heard from Evelyn, Bob's wife. I was going to tell him."

"Thanks," Hinkle said sarcastically. "Any messages you have, just deliver 'em through the sheriff, here."

"Bob! Don't be like that."

"Any of you folks hear anything of the car being driven away?" Selby asked.

They glanced at each other, shook their heads.

"Where you working?" Brandon asked Hinkle.

"For the Leasehold Consolidated Oil Company."

"How long you been with them?"

"About two months."

"You say you're divorced?"

"My wife left me."

"When?"

"About two weeks after we got here. She went to Reno to get a divorce. I guess she's got it now."

"And you're keeping this house by yourself?"

"I'm staying on until I can find a room somewhere. I'm leaving next week."

"Your car a 1939 Pontiac sedan?"

"That's right."

"Did you leave the ignition unlocked?"

Hinkle scratched his head again. "I guess I did. How bad was the bus smashed?"

"It's all wrapped around the steering wheel."

Hinkle said, "Cripes, I let my insurance lapse after the wife walked out! Of all the bum luck!"

Brandon looked at Selby.

Selby said, "Well, we're just checking up. The car's over in Madison City – what's left of it. You can take a look at it any time in the morning."

"I'll be working," Hinkle said. He turned to Grines. "S'pose you and Ruth can take a run over to see what can be done?"

"Sure," Grines said. "We'll drive you to work in the morning, and then go over and take a look."

Selby said, "I'll want to talk with Mr and Mrs Grines again after we've made a more detailed investigation. Sorry we bothered you, but we were checking up. We wanted to find who was driving the car."

Back in the county car Billy Ransome said, "Well, that's service, all right. We find a man's car before he knows it's been stolen ... Why all the commotion about it, Sheriff?"

Brandon said, "Apparently, it was being driven by Desmond Billmeyer, the chain store grocer ... Tell you what you do, Ransome. Get a line on Hinkle in the morning and find out everything you can about Grines. Ask the Leasehold Consolidated people what kind of a worker Hinkle is, and how he's doing, will you?"

"Okay. Want me to telephone you?"

"Yes, if you will, please."

They dropped Ransome at his house and drove on to Madison City, arriving there shortly before three-fifteen. The city looked utterly deserted. Only the towering smokestacks and lighted buildings of the beet sugar factory showed any sign of activity.

"Looks like a good crop of sugar beets this year," Brandon Selby yawned sleepily. "Also a good crop of murders ... See you at nine o'clock, Rex."

The Friday morning *Clarion* carried the story under headlines:

WEALTHY BUSINESSMAN KILLED HERE
SWIFT ACTION BY COUNTY AUTHORITIES RESULTS IN IDENTIFICATION – BAFFLING CIRCUMSTANCES SURROUND MYSTERIOUS DEATH – SHERIFF AND DISTRICT ATTORNEY SPEED INVESTIGATION

Selby read the article at breakfast. By the time he reached his office, Amorette Standish, his secretary, reported there had been several calls from Los Angeles. Selby had hardly entered his private office before the phone rang. The city editor of a Los Angeles daily wanted an interview. He seemed politely sceptical concerning the identification, and Selby, retiring into the shell of his official dignity, stated merely that the body had been identified by two persons who knew the executive, and that his office was conducting an investigation into the circumstances surrounding his death.

Brandon came in shortly after, and a few moments later they were joined by Dr Trueman. The autopsy surgeon looked crisply professional, and, as a good doctor should, gave no indication of having been up all night.

"Well," Selby asked, "what did you find?"

Dr Trueman spoke slowly, deliberately. "I found a man of approximately forty-two years of age. He had been drinking heavily. The auto accident didn't cause his death. He had a bad heart, and quite probably didn't even know it. He had probably led a normally active life without experiencing any particular inconvenience other than of late an occasional shortness of breath. If he'd lived three years longer, he'd have had more serious symptoms.

"I would say, however, death was due to a heart failure which, in turn, was superinduced by a dose of chloral hydrate."

"Knockout drops?" Selby asked.

"Generally so called," Dr Trueman said. "And when a person has a weak heart, a large dose is dangerous. Chloral hydrate isn't too easy to detect, but I have satisfied myself that a considerable quantity was administered, and that death occurred soon after the drug was ingested."

"How do you know that?" Selby asked.

Dr Trueman said, "It happens to be one of the things I'm up on. A man by the name of Archangelsky has made exhaustive tests showing that chloral hydrate is not uniformly distributed in the blood. At the inception of the narcosis, there is less drug in the brain than in the blood. Later on, this situation reverses itself. I found a greater percentage in the blood than in the brain. Therefore, I conclude death intervened before the drug had reached its maximum efficiency; in other words, relatively soon after its administration.

"I was able to recover enough of the liquor which had soaked the clothing from the broken flask to determine there was chloral hydrate in it. I couldn't tell how much."

"Is there," Selby asked, "any possibility this chloral hydrate was self-administered?"

"Yes, there's a possibility."

"How strong a possibility?"

"As to that I'm not prepared to say. That's out of my field as an expert. It's pure speculation. Chloral hydrate is used occasionally as a hypnotic. I've known of persons taking it voluntarily when they found themselves recovering from the after-effects of an acute alcoholism."

"What the layman would call a hold-over?" Selby asked, smiling.

Dr Trueman nodded.

"What did you find out about the time of death, Doctor?"

"That's always a difficult question. I would say that death occurred about nine o'clock, but to be on the safe side, you'd have to say between eight-thirty and nine-thirty. I think I can place it within those time limits and stand up under cross-examination."

"Just how do you fix the time?" Selby asked.

"A variety of factors. Understand, Doug, I don't want to seem unduly technical, but you're asking these questions. We've got to go into them sooner or later, and you may as well know what I'm working on … There are two deaths: somatic death and molecular death. In other words, after a person is dead, his individual tissues and cells will still react to various stimuli for a certain period. Taking all of this into consideration, judging the time of onset of rigor mortis, constructing a temperature curve of body cooling, I would say that death occurred at approximately nine o'clock."

Selby said, "All right, Doctor, thanks a lot. I think you've given me everything I need."

When Dr Trueman had gone, Selby said, "Let's not kid ourselves, Rex. We've got a murder case on our hands. Let's – " He looked up as Amorette Standish opened the door.

"Mr J C Gillespie wants to know if he can see you."

"Send him in."

Gillespie, a man in the early fifties with iron-grey hair and a close-cropped moustache, was carrying a folded *Clarion* in his left hand. He advanced to Selby's desk with the direct manner of a man who is accustomed to getting things done quickly.

"You're Selby," he said. "I met you two years ago – shortly after I came to Madison City. You may not remember me. Sheriff Brandon I've seen more recently. Good morning, gentlemen."

There was a crisp businesslike efficiency in Mr Gillespie's manner, a biting off of the words as though he wished to get to the point as quickly as possible.

Selby shook hands. "Won't you sit down?"

Gillespie spread out *The Clarion*. "How much truth," he demanded, "is there to this?"

"To what?"

"About Desmond Billmeyer."

Selby glanced at Brandon, then said, "The article is substantially correct."

"The identification was positive?"

"Absolutely. There can be no question."

Gillespie's breath came out in a sigh of resignation. "Well, that's that. I'd been trying to convince myself it must have been a newspaper exaggeration. I couldn't believe it – didn't seem possible."

He gnawed at the ends of his moustache. "Humph. Strange – damn strange. A shock – devil of a shock ... Hang it, men, I had an appointment with Desmond Billmeyer. I worried all night over his failure to show up."

"What time was your appointment?"

"Nothing exactly definite. He was coming in to see me. It was a real estate transaction. Stephen Freelman was the agent. Billmeyer's most trusted assistant had recently married Stephen Freelman's brother ... Billmeyer thought there might be some question of ethics in case he dealt directly with Freelman. He wanted to get the price whittled down to the last cent. I thought he was leaning over backwards; but he wanted me to purchase the property on the best deal I could, and I finally agreed to do so. I was, of course, doing it as a favour to him – without profit – acting as his agent – well, dummy, if you want to call it that."

Selby glanced at Brandon and withheld comment.

"Desmond was all ready to close," Gillespie went on. "I'd got Stephen Freelman's principals down to what I considered was absolutely the lowest price obtainable. I called Desmond and told him so … He'd asked me to call him just as soon as I'd concluded my interview."

"Where did you call him?" Selby asked.

"At a Hollywood number. He said he'd be waiting there all the afternoon."

"What time was it when you called?"

"Oh, I don't know. Around six o'clock, I guess; perhaps six-thirty. I didn't notice the time exactly. Freelman was still at my house talking. He didn't leave until around seven. I stepped into another room to put through the call. I told Desmond the price. He seemed elated, but told me to raise certain objections which would have the effect of sending Freelman back to look over the property. He said he'd come in to see me right away and bring an amount sufficient to start an escrow."

"Did he say how much?"

"No, gentlemen, he didn't, but the property involved was selling at – well, suppose we say somewhere in the neighbourhood of a hundred thousand dollars."

"Go ahead," Selby said.

"I kept waiting and waiting. Desmond didn't show up. That wasn't like him. He was usually very prompt. I didn't go to bed until after one o'clock. I tried ringing Desmond's office several times, but got no answer … Then this morning I read this in the paper.

"Hang it, gentlemen, it's impossible. It's preposterous! Desmond under the influence of liquor! The man never touched a drop. I know that for a fact."

"How long," Selby asked, "have you known him?"

"Seven or eight years."

"Intimately?"

"Intimately for five years."

"Did you," Selby asked, "ever hear him speak of a man by the name of Grines?"

"I don't think so. Of course, he might have. I have a hard time remembering names myself. You know, people whom I meet … I could hardly be expected to remember a name which was mentioned in casual conversation, but the name doesn't sound at all familiar … May I ask why you inquire?"

Selby said guardedly, "I thought that Billmeyer might have had some contact with a man named Grines – oh, some time ago."

"Or perhaps very recently," Sheriff Brandon supplemented.

"Can't say that I remember ever hearing him mention the name," Gillespie said. "Who was he? A businessman? Associate or – "

"We don't know yet," Selby said. "We're investigating."

Mr Gillespie got to his feet. "Shocking," he said. "Knocked me all in a heap. Couldn't eat a bite of breakfast."

Selby said, "If you were intimately acquainted with him, we'd like very much to have you go down to Perkins' place and look at the body."

Gillespie bristled. "Hang it, gentlemen, I thought you said there was no question about it."

"There isn't," Selby said. "The body was identified by Mrs Gilbert Freelman as being that of Billmeyer."

"But," Selby went on, "we'd like to check up on Mrs Freelman."

Gillespie's eyes narrowed. "I'm not certain that I understand – No, no, I don't want to. I was going to ask you – even if you hadn't suggested it – if it would be all right for me to take a look at the body … Something strange, gentlemen. If Desmond Billmeyer had been drinking, someone forced him to take the liquor. I'm willing to be quoted on that – absolutely … I understand from the paper there are some so-called mysterious circumstances."

Selby's only answer was a nod.

His caller hesitated as though starting to say something, then, apparently thinking better of it, started for the door. "I'll look at the body, gentlemen. Do you wish me to call you?"

"If you will, please."

"I'll go right down."

He got as far as the door, then paused, fidgeting uneasily.

"Was there," Selby asked, getting to his feet and moving around his desk, "something else?"

Gillespie cleared his throat. "Don't know whether you know it," he said. "Few people did. Of course, you may have stumbled onto it in your investigations. There's a hiatus in Desmond Billmeyer's life. He never spoke of it. In fact has gone to the other extreme, trying to cover it up by inventing a historical background. Purely fictitious."

"What do you mean?" Selby asked.

"He had a complete loss of memory. I knew him for years before he told me anything about it. I think the thought preyed on his mind, haunted him. He told me once that he thought his past life contained a dark chapter that had to do with drink and with a burning building; said that he woke up at nights in a perspiration, dreaming of a burning building. He also had a feeling that if he ever started drinking, he'd let himself go – lose all control. I know he talked it over with me in detail one night; said that he sometimes thought he might bring back the memory of his earlier life if he submitted to hypnotism, but he was afraid to do it. And I warned him against it."

"Why?" Selby asked.

Gillespie shook his head. "I have ideas of my own about amnesia. When you're suffering such intense pain that you can't face it, you faint. That's nature's way of escape. Whenever you lose consciousness, it's because the consciousness wants to be lost. Same way with memory, gentlemen. You forget your past life when that seems to be the only way out. When you're ready to regain your memory, you'll get it back. That's my philosophy, gentlemen."

"Did you," Selby asked, his voice edged with interest, "tell Billmeyer your ideas about that?"

Gillespie said positively, "I most certainly did. I told him to leave well enough alone. He was highly successful, a good businessman, well liked by his friends, respected in the community, a driving, aggressive type of executive."

He took a deep breath. "Hope I haven't told you too much, gentlemen. It's betraying a confidence. However, if he'd been drinking, there's something radically wrong. You should know it."

Selby said, "I think, Mr Gillespie, you may have given us something that is highly significant."

"Well, I hope so. I wouldn't have spoken about it otherwise. I'll go down and see that body. It must be Desmond. He'd have kept that appointment last night if he'd been physically able. The property was something he wanted *very* much. It represented a key to certain plans he had for expanding his business."

"And that may have had something to do with his desire to keep his name out of it?" Selby asked. "In other words, his objections to dealing with Freelman weren't all ethical?"

Gillespie glanced shrewdly at the district attorney. "He didn't *say* so. I, of course, drew certain conclusions. He owned pieces on each side of this property. He would have been a logical purchaser. Freelman called Desmond when the piece he was handling first went on the market. Billmeyer told him he wasn't interested. Rather shrewd, that. Billmeyer even said he'd sell his adjoining pieces if he could get a fair price. Sort of put the price down that way … Billmeyer was shrewd all right."

"He wasn't, by any chance, carrying that money in cash, was he?" Selby asked.

"He may have been. He was as anxious to get that deal closed as Freelman's clients were. Incidentally, Stephen Freelman was depending on this commission very strongly. He let that slip … Of course, gentlemen, you understand that all of this I've told you is to be in the most sacred confidence."

Selby nodded.

"Particularly that part about the loss of memory. That isn't for the press. Don't want to cheapen my friend's memory. He told me I was the only living soul he'd ever discussed it with. Said I talked his language. He wasn't the sort who opened up easily … Hang it, gentlemen, there's a limit to these things. I know you have to investigate such matters, and that means prying into a person's life to some extent, but there's a limit, a very definite limit, particularly so far as the press is concerned."

Selby, who had followed Mr Gillespie to the door, extended his hand. "I think you've been a very material help, and you can rest assured we'll do whatever we can to protect your confidence."

When the door had closed, Selby looked at Brandon and pursed his lips in a low whistle.

Brandon fished a cloth sack of tobacco out of his pocket. "There," he said, "is the explanation. Something made Billmeyer take a drink. When he got drunk he remembered who he was and forgot he was Billmeyer."

"And that dormant personality," Selby said, "was – "

"That of Carleton Grines, a crook," Brandon finished.

"And," Selby went on musingly, "when the thing clicked in his consciousness, his mind went back exactly ten years. He remembered where he'd left the suit of clothes he'd taken off ten years ago. He got that suit, picked up the thread of his life where he'd dropped it ten years ago – and got murdered as a result."

Brandon spilled rattling tobacco grains into the cupped paper. "And what a sweet spot that leaves us in," he said. "We've got to start running down a trail that's ten years old, the evidence locked in the dead brain of a corpse."

Selby pulled a pipe from his pocket. "Well, Rex," he said, "we've got one thing to work on. The most significant clue of all."

"What's that?"

"When Billmeyer's mind clicked back to that occasion ten years ago when something had happened that had brought on the amnesia and he remembered where he'd left his clothes, he went to that place, *and the clothes were still there.*"

Brandon looked up from his half-rolled cigarette. "By gosh, son," he said, "you got somethin'. You got somethin' there for a fact."

CHAPTER SEVEN

It was nine-forty-five when Alphonse Baker Carr called on Selby. With him was a young man who seemed to have an explosive personality and a chip on his shoulder.

A B Carr was very definitely an outstanding personality, a man who could enter a room and, by the very manner of his entrance, claim the attention of every person within that room. A big-time criminal lawyer who had established statewide fame in his profession, he had purchased a pretentious house in Madison City where, as he said, he wanted "to get away from it all."

But the legal services of Old ABC, as he was affectionately called by the type of clients who referred to an attorney as a "mouthpiece," were apparently only the more in demand as the old maestro tried to retire.

There were those who said Carr had come to Madison City because he was pursued by the fear that his connection with the underworld had grown into a Frankenstein monster, or, as the Chinese would have expressed it, he was riding a tiger and could not dismount. These persons whispered that some day Carr would mysteriously disappear, and no one would ever know whether he had quietly faded into voluntary oblivion or had been "taken for a ride." These people claimed that establishing a residence in Madison City was the first step to carry out Carr's plan for a mysterious disappearance.

Whatever the reason, his presence had proven embarrassing. Neighbours told of expensive automobiles purring up to Carr's residence in the dead of night, of mysterious lights which came and went in the windows of the house, of low voiced conferences audible on warm nights through the open windows.

Had Carr gone on the stage he would have achieved outstanding success. The man, in fact, seemed more like an actor than an attorney, due in part to his keen sense of the dramatic and his ability to exploit it.

Carr made a little inclusive gesture with his hand, and, by that gesture, managed to bring the young man who accompanied him into the picture as a major character. It was as though the gesture invested his youthful companion with some of Carr's magnetic personality.

"Selby, I don't think you've met Milton Gregory."

Selby acknowledged the introduction, then turned inquiringly to Carr.

Carr, in the firm but kindly tone one would use in giving a command to a high-strung horse, said, "Sit down, Milton." Carr also sat down, crossed one long leg over the other and fished a cigar from his pocket with the calm assurance of one settling himself for a visit.

Selby looked at his watch. "You'll have to be brief. I have an important appointment in fifteen minutes."

Carr carefully snipped the end from the cigar, regarded it speculatively, and by that little gesture managed to emphasize the significance of his remark as he said, "Mr Gregory is a brother of Carmen Gregory, who is now Carmen Freelman."

Selby sensing what was to come, managed a noncommittal, "Indeed," and then added, "my appointment is with Mrs Freelman."

"That," Carr said, "is what we wanted to see you about," and, having made that announcement, deliberately took time out to light a match and hold it to the end of his cigar.

Selby concealed his irritation. "What about it?"

Milton Gregory said, "What about it! Good heavens, you've – "

Carr's left hand came up, palm outward, and something in the impressive, graceful gesture dried up the impending torrent of words. "Now, Milton," Old ABC said in a voice that was calm and unhurried, but with a deeply resonant timbre which made it more effective than would have been the shout of an ordinary man, "you're paying me to do your talking …" He smiled at Selby. "So many clients," he said conversationally, "employ an attorney and then want to do the talking themselves."

Selby said, "I don't care which one of you does the talking, only get started." He realized as soon as the words had left his mouth how impatient his voice had sounded. Old ABC was a past-master at stealing the show. He was even now putting himself in command of the situation.

Carr said, "Unfortunately, Carmen Freelman won't be here this morning."

"Unfortunately for her," Selby said, fighting hard to keep from losing his temper.

Carr made a deprecating gesture. "As you wish."

At that moment Sheriff Brandon opened the door, said, "Hello, Doug. Has Carmen Freelman showed up?" And then, seeing Carr, "Good morning, Carr."

Selby said, "Rex, this is Milton Gregory, Carmen Freelman's brother. He has evidently employed A B Carr to see that Carmen Freelman doesn't keep her appointment this morning."

Brandon's face flushed. "All right," he said to Carr, "now I'll tell you the answer to that. We've been pretty patient with you, but if you think you can pull the tricks here you pull in the city – "

Selby said, placatingly, "Just a minute, Rex. Let's find out first just where we stand. I think you'll admit, Carr, that we could have gone ahead with an examination of Mrs Freelman last night – probably should have done so."

Carr smiled. "That was last night. Since then she's had a nervous breakdown."

Selby said, "That alibi has whiskers growing halfway to the floor."

"That, gentlemen," Carr said, "is your strongest assurance that she actually *has* had a nervous breakdown. Please give me credit for enough ingenuity to have thought up something more plausible had I been resorting to falsehood."

Selby said, "Or to have used the time-honoured device and freshened it up with a speech such as that."

Carr made him a little bow. "Thank you, Counsellor," he said. "You have expressed it admirably."

Abruptly Selby laughed. "May I ask where Mrs Freelman is?" he asked.

"Why, certainly," Carr said. "Of course."

"Where?"

"She's in a sanitarium under the care of her physician."

"And where is that sanitarium?"

Carr's long fingers stroked the angle of his lean jaw. "Well now, gentlemen, *that's* different. Her husband accompanied – "

Young Gregory said, "And if there's any further attempt made to hound – "

"Tut, tut, my young friend," Carr said. "There you go again."

"Well, that's all right. I'm entitled to say something."

"You certainly are," Carr said, getting to his feet. "Go right ahead, say whatever you want. Of course, since you're going to do the talking, you won't need me, so I'll wish you a good morning."

Gregory said sulkily, "I didn't mean it that way."

Carr stood looking down at him. "Well, I did."

"Come back and sit down," Gregory said sheepishly. "I won't say anything more."

"There's nothing to sit down about," Brandon said angrily. "You've spirited this woman away so we can't question her. Now,

I'm going to tell you something. There's enough evidence here to drag her name into publicity which is going to hurt. We've been trying to keep her out of it."

Carr said suavely, "Very thoughtful of you. Do you know, Sheriff, I can't help but contrast the way the officials of this county prosecute cases and the manner used in the larger cities. There, almost any expedient is used to get publicity ... Come on, Milton. We'll be going."

Brandon moved between Carr and the door. "Just a minute," he said. "You haven't told us where Carmen is yet."

"That's right," ABC said, "I haven't."

"And you don't intend to?" the sheriff asked.

"No."

"You took her to a sanitarium?" Selby asked.

Carr's mobile eyebrows elevated slowly. "*I* took her to a sanitarium?" he echoed, with every indication of surprised incredulity. "Good Heavens! Mrs Freelman, gentlemen, is under the care of a physician."

"Would you mind giving me the name of that physician?"

"Dr Lewis A Rapp of Los Angeles."

"Also a client of yours, I suppose?"

Carr said thoughtfully, "Let me see ... Yes, I *have* done work for Dr Rapp ... I guess you might say that he was a client of mine."

"You accompanied her to the sanitarium?"

"I haven't discussed the facts with her, if that's what you're trying to get at. Dr Rapp told me that she was in no condition to discuss the case with anyone. Under those circumstances there was nothing for *me* to do except await her recovery."

Carr again started for the door. Milton Gregory moved up close to the lawyer's side. Carr turned as he opened the door, bowed, and contrived to make their exit a triumphant march off the stage.

When the door had closed, Selby met the consternation in Brandon's eyes. "You know what this means, son," the sheriff said. "We had her in our hands, and we let her slip right through them. The taxpayers aren't going to like that – unless we do something about it – pronto."

CHAPTER EIGHT

Sylvia Martin came in about eleven.

"Busy, Doug?"

"Not too busy to talk with you."

"I hear Carmen Freelman took a run-out powder."

Selby nodded.

"Why?"

"I wish I knew ... How did you find out?"

"Oh, I've been down at the sheriff's office snooping around for news. He told me ... Have you called the doctor, Doug?"

Selby laughed and said, "Not yet. It's really a waste of money on a long distance telephone bill. He'll either be very suave and courteous or short and crusty. In either event the outcome will be the same."

"Hear anything from the Los Angeles papers, Doug?"

"One city editor called me, seemed rather sceptical about the whole business."

She said, "I've sent in the story. Things will be humming by night. How's the case coming?"

Selby lit up his pipe, and Sylvia watched the keen eyes, the long, straight nose and firm lips as the light of the match flickered them into reddish illumination.

Selby blew out the match. "Think the opposition newspaper will take a poke at me for letting Carmen slip through my fingers?"

"Will it! *The Blade* will run an editorial about the lax methods used in the county offices that will curl your hair."

Selby grinned. "You and I," he said, "are going to find Carmen."

"How, Doug?"

"By using a little ingenuity to run down a clue no one has even thought about."

"What?"

"Her husband, Gilbert Freelman, drove her out to the sanitarium. Old ABC let that slip."

"But you can't make *him* tell – "

"I'm not going to try to make *him* tell, but perhaps his automobile will tell. He had his car serviced at the Standard station on the corner yesterday morning. The attendant must have made a check of the speedometer.

"Now then, Carmen Freelman went to the Hollywood office yesterday afternoon for a conference with Billmeyer. She got back around eleven-forty-five. In round figures, we can call it seventy miles from here to Hollywood, so that trip will put one hundred and forty miles on the speedometer. Gilbert drove his wife up to the coroner's and back. That will account for approximately six miles more. Almost immediately after Carr left my office I went out to Freelman's ranch. I wanted to talk with Gilbert and persuade him his wife was making a mistake."

"Did you?"

Selby shook his head. "They said he was asleep, that he'd been up nearly all night, that he was very much worried about his wife. The doctor had given him some sleeping tablets to take and left word he wasn't to be awakened.

"His car was standing in the yard, so I looked it over. The gasoline tank was almost empty, so I took the speedometer reading. It was nine thousand six hundred and fifty-one miles.

"The coroner is going to get that earlier speedometer reading from the service station."

"That may be a clue," she said. "I saw Corliss Ditmer on the street this morning. She seems put out at Carmen. She said that, after all, Carmen had nothing to conceal, that Billmeyer telephoned her just as they were sitting down to dinner yesterday, that he was working and couldn't find some letters. He made her go in all the way to Hollywood to open the files and find them."

"Then what happened?" Selby asked. "Did Carmen come right back?"

"Corliss said that Carmen wasn't exactly definite about it, but she gathered that Billmeyer had kept her for a conference about an important matter of business … Well, let me know if you learn anything from the speedometer."

Almost as soon as Sylvia left, Amorette Standish opened the door and said, "The coroner's here."

"Send him in," Selby said.

Harry Perkins came striding into the room. "How goes it, Doug?"

Selby grinned. "So-so. What's new with you?"

Perkins said, "The speedometer reading was nine thousand four hundred and ninety-nine – and I've got a dog on my hands. He didn't belong to the people in that car, after all."

"Why, he was in there with the children. I – "

"I know," Perkins said, "but he isn't their dog. I took him over to where the children were staying. They'd gone to the hospital, so I left Fido with the owner of the auto camp. He said he'd see the kids got him soon as they came back. He telephoned a few minutes ago and said to come and get my dog. The kids had never seen him before."

"He *must* be their dog," Selby said.

"Nope. He doesn't belong to them. He growled at the kids."

Selby thought for a moment. "Well, I guess you've got a dog."

Selby's long-distance telephone call to the Oregon authorities came through shortly before noon. When he had explained who he was and what he wanted to know, the man at the other end of the line said, "Yes, I remember perfectly. In fact, I was on duty at the time. It was January 21st, 1932. There was a prison riot. Somehow, the prisoners had got hold of guns. Half a dozen escaped before a posse got the place surrounded. Then the thing caught fire. No one knows whether the fire was set by the prisoners or by some overzealous member of the posse. The prisoners had taken possession of the jail.

"After the fire started, we called on them to come out with their hands up, and promised we wouldn't shoot. They wouldn't come out. When they finally decided to break through, it was too late. About half of them were trapped when the roof collapsed."

"How about a man named Carleton Grines?" Selby asked.

"He was one of the prisoners who burned to death. He had a brother living in Oklahoma. I remember the occasion well. The brother claimed we had deliberately held out on him."

"Wasn't there some delay?" Selby insisted.

"Of course, there was a delay. The ringleader wouldn't give us the names of the persons who were with him in the burning prison because he didn't want us to find out which ones had escaped. Most of the bodies were burnt beyond recognition. We never did get the mess straightened out until we recaptured some of the prisoners who had escaped. They told us some of the ones who had been with them. Finally, the ringleader gave us a complete list, but that was a long while later. We notified this man's brother just as soon as we had the information ourselves. You'd have thought we'd deliberately killed his brother, the way he acted."

"What was Carleton Grines in for?"

"I've forgotten. I can look it up, in case you want to know. All of our records were burned up in the fire, but the court records, showing his conviction and sentence, are still available. I'll look 'em up and send you the information if it's that important."

Selby said, "I'd like to have them, thanks."

The phone rang again as soon as he had hung up. Brandon on the line announced that Pervis Grines and his wife were down looking at the wreckage of Hinkle's car, and had decided there was no use trying to repair it, that it would have to be junked.

Selby said, "Get hold of them, Rex, and have them taken down to Perkins' place. I want to have them look at that body."

Brandon said, "I'll meet you there in ten minutes."

Seen by daylight, Pervis Grines was a slim man in the early thirties. He carried himself with his. shoulders back, his chin up, moving with lithe, athletic grace. His thick, full lips indicated an emotional nature, and marred an otherwise attractive face. He was carrying a folded *Clarion* under his arm.

Mrs Grines, blonde and good-looking, had a free and easy friendliness of manner which enabled her to minimize her husband's occasional fits of truculence.

Selby opened the closet where the rough suit of tweeds had been hung. "Remember ever having seen a suit of that sort?" he asked.

Pervis Grines started to shake his head, then arrested the shake almost at its inception to stare in frowning concentration at the clothes.

Mrs Grines answered the question. "Why, Pervis, Carleton had a suit just like that! Remember when he left Cherokee Flats right after we were married? Pervis, he was wearing a suit just like that."

"Not that same suit," Pervis said. "It might have been one that looked like it."

She said, "I'll bet it was that same suit."

"Let's see that envelope," Selby said to Perkins.

The coroner handed it to him.

Selby showed Pervis the envelope addressed to Carleton Grines, General Delivery, Phoenix, Arizona.

"Is that," he asked, "your writing?"

Grines' face flushed. "How did you get that?" he demanded.

Selby, watching him closely, said quietly, "It was in the inside pocket of the coat this man was wearing."

"That's an envelope I addressed to my brother ten years ago. I – I'd got him out of some trouble, and it took every cent we could scrape up. Ruth and I had just been married, and we'd been counting on that for a little nest egg ... He had to get out of the state, and we agreed I was to write him at General Delivery, Phoenix, Arizona. I told him that as far as I was concerned, I was washing my hands of him."

"He was always getting into trouble," Mrs Grines supplemented.

"What sort of trouble?"

"Driving while he was drunk," "Grines blurted. "He was always getting liquored and driving his automobile. When he had a few drinks under his belt, he'd push the throttle all the way down and go like the very devil.

"He'd been caught three or four times before he had this big accident. He promised he'd quit driving when he'd been drinking. He couldn't do it. He just couldn't control himself where liquor was concerned."

Mrs Grines fingered the material in the tweed suit. She turned to Selby. "He'd been wearing this suit about four months before he left Cherokee Flats. It was beginning to look just a little seedy ... I remember him plain as day, the way he used to come calling on us, trying to get Pervis to help him out of his scrape, and the way he'd treat me. You wouldn't think that *I* had anything to say about the money. He'd kid me along until he could get Pervis off to one side. If he'd only come out frankly and – Where did you get that suit?"

Pervis said, "That's what I want to know. How did this guy manage to get my brother's clothes?"

Selby said, "Let's take a look at the body. That may answer your question."

Harry Perkins pulled out a long drawer-like affair.

It was Mrs Grines' quick gasp which told Selby what he wanted to know, even before Pervis Grines said, "That's him – that's Carleton. He's changed in ten years, put on a lot of weight, and his face isn't the same – looks more determined ... And I thought he'd been dead ten years ... So he got tanked up again and finally got his. Poor kid! So *he* was Billmeyer!"

Mrs Grines said, "Well, he left enough so he can pay us what he borrowed ten years ago."

Pervis stared at her. "Good gosh," he said, "we might get it *all*. They say he was a big shot."

Selby watched them closely.

They looked dazed, then Pervis said, "Poor old Carl."

"Don't be a hypocrite," his wife said sharply. Then to Selby, "How much was he worth?"

"At the very least, half a million," Selby said.

Selby, Sylvia Martin, and Rex Brandon gathered around the desk in the district attorney's office.

Selby said, "I read the speedometer on Gilbert Freelman's automobile this morning. It showed nine thousand six hundred and fifty-one miles. Perkins got the speedometer reading of yesterday morning when Freelman had his car serviced. It was nine thousand four hundred and ninety-nine."

Brandon did mental arithmetic. "Let's see, about a hundred and fifty miles."

"Exactly one hundred and fifty-two miles," Selby said. "Now that car made a trip to Hollywood, went to Harry Perkins' office when we had her identify the body; and went to this sanitarium Old ABC is talking about."

Brandon nodded.

Sylvia Martin pulled a pencil from her purse and did some rapid figuring.

Selby said, "We call it a hundred and forty miles from here to Hollywood and back in round figures. The Freelman ranch is about three miles out of town."

"That doesn't leave much for the sanitarium trip," Brandon observed, puzzled.

"That's just it," Selby said. "Our sanitarium must be right here in Madison City."

Rex Brandon puckered his forehead.

"I get it," Sylvia said. "It's just about the distance from the Freelman ranch to the outskirts of town and back – probably to Orange Heights."

"Exactly," Selby said, "and what sanitarium is there on Orange Heights?"

Brandon looked at Sylvia Martin, said, "Shucks, son, there ain't any."

Selby nodded. "On Orange Heights," he said, "there is only one place which would have furnished sanctuary for a person who was trying to avoid an interview with the officers of the law."

"The residence of A B Carr," Sylvia said.

Brandon said slowly with an interval of pause between each word, "Well, I'll – be – doggoned."

Sylvia Martin said, "I've got something else for you, Doug, something I ran onto by accident. After Gilbert and Carmen Freelman left Perkins' undertaking parlours, they stopped at a gas station and had the tank filled up. It was an all-night station on the boulevard, and the attendant noticed that Carmen had been crying. He overheard scraps of the conversation. He remembers Gilbert said to her almost angrily, 'Carmen, why didn't you tell me this before?' and she sobbed out, 'I was afraid to.' Then they saw the service station attendant standing by the door, cleaning off the windshield wing, and they became suddenly silent."

Selby pulled his pipe from his pocket and started cramming tobacco down in the bowl. "Well," he said, "we've got something for you, Sylvia. We've finally got the body identified. It's Carleton Grines."

Her face showed dismay. "Oh, Doug! Then it isn't – wasn't Billmeyer, and you've been so positive – "

"Wait a minute, sister," Rex Brandon drawled. "The body is also that of Billmeyer."

"You mean that – "

"That Carleton Grines and Desmond Billmeyer were one and the same person."

Selby said, "Apparently the pieces of the puzzle fit together like this: Grines was a heavy drinker. He had a habit of getting liquored up and driving a car. He left Oklahoma in disgrace. His brother, who had previously stood by him, got disgusted and decided to quit putting up. Carleton went to Oregon and was arrested. There was a jail break. During the break, someone set fire to the jail. The roof collapsed. Quite a few prisoners were killed. Several of the bodies were burned beyond identification. The authorities thought that Carleton Grines had been killed in the fire. Evidently he had managed to escape from the burning building. Probably something fell on his head, inflicting an injury which brought on a case of what the doctors call traumatic amnesia.

"He started life all over again, not knowing who he was, but having two fears deeply embedded in his subconscious mind. One of them was a fear of drink, and the other a horror of being trapped in a burning building. He went into the grocery business and saved his wages. He got credit backing and opened a store of his own. Then he bought out more stores and – "

"I know the story of his success," Sylvia interrupted. "I've been doing some research work on it, digging out everything I could find, but I thought – Why, he gives a complete biographical background."

Selby said, "Because he was always afraid of whatever ghost might rise up from the past to confront him with something disagreeable."

Sylvia said, "Doug, what a *whale* of a story!"

Selby said, "You haven't heard all of it yet. Something happened on Thanksgiving night. Evidently, he started drinking. As he began to get intoxicated, the memory of his past came to him. In all probability, the ten-year interval during which he had been Desmond Billmeyer slipped from his mind, and he became only Carleton Grines, anxious to return to Oklahoma City to call on his brother.

"Now then, somewhere he had left the suit of clothes he had worn when he left Oklahoma. The clothes didn't fit him any more, because he'd put on quite a bit of weight, but the point is, he knew where those clothes were; and the significant thing is, those clothes had remained undisturbed over the ten-year period."

"And he became overcome with remorse and called the sheriff?" Sylvia asked.

Selby shook his head. "The man had been dead for an hour and a half when Brandon received that call."

"Doug, that isn't right. That can't be right."

"Why?"

She said, "Dr Trueman must have made a mistake somehow. It would have been so logical for Carleton Grines to have done that very thing. It – it fits into the picture too well."

Selby said, "Dr Trueman's positive."

"Then there's something wrong in his facts. Getting drunk, driving the car, getting a crying jag, and calling the sheriff, and then, before the sheriff got there, starting away in the car … It's absolutely typical of Carleton Grines' character, as you've painted it, Doug."

Selby frowned down into the tobacco smoke.

Sylvia Martin said, "When people realize the facts of this case, it's going to push you so far out in the limelight you'll feel like moths in the beam of a searchlight. If there's anything you want to do quietly, you'd better do it before this breaks."

Selby grinned. "There's lots we want to do, but we don't know what it is."

Brandon nodded. "Like a guy on a buckin' horse," he said. "He's busy as hell – just sittin' there."

CHAPTER NINE

Ma Freelman was dry-eyed but only because she had been raised in a school of life where women accomplish nothing through tears, only through work, faith, courage and persistence.

She said, "Mr Selby, I'm in trouble. I'd been pridin' myself that we'd raised such good boys, and they'd been so successful, an' now – " She swallowed hard and said wearily, "and now this comes! Of course, you can't blame Gilbert for standing back of her. That's his duty. She's his wife."

Selby nodded sympathetically.

"Where," he asked, "is Gilbert?"

"The doctor gave Gilbert something to make him sleep. He left word Gilbert wasn't to be disturbed. When you were out there this morning, I wouldn't let them call him 'cause I thought he'd come to see you as soon as he woke up ... Well, he didn't."

"Where did he go?"

"He jumped in his car and drove off. I think he went to see that lawyer."

"A B Carr?"

"Yes."

"And then what?"

"He hasn't come back."

"What time did Gilbert get back after he took Carmen to that sanitarium?"

"Not until after daylight. He said Carmen was where no one could disturb her. He was awfully hard to talk to, sort of deaf-like. He had some tablets the doctor had given him to take as soon as he got home. He was awful jittery, Mr Selby. I've never seen one of my boys like that."

"Billmeyer called her during Thanksgiving dinner?" Selby asked.

"Just when we started eating. That was about two o'clock. Then they called her again after that. It was after that second call she said she had to go … That first call upset her a lot, though. I know that. Of course, I don't *know* who either call was from. They were just long distance."

Selby said, "All right, Mrs Freelman, go back home. When you see Gilbert, tell him that if I don't hear from him I'll take it as an admission his wife is guilty of some crime."

Mrs Freelman got up, said, "Thank you, Mr Selby. Just talkin' to you makes a body feel better, somehow."

Selby saw her to the door, then came to sit on the edge of his desk, puffing thoughtfully at his pipe. After a few moments he picked up the telephone and told the courthouse operator to get him the sheriff's office. When Brandon was on the line, he said, "I've just had a talk with Mrs Freelman, Rex."

"Carmen?"

"No. Gilbert's mother. She said something that's given me a clue. Are you where I can talk with you, Rex?"

"Yes. I'm alone in the private office. I'm reading the editorial in *The Blade*. Have you seen it?"

Selby said, "No. I'm coming down. I'll read it in your office and then tell you my story."

Selby walked down to the door of Brandon's private office. There was an angry glitter in the sheriff's eyes as he handed the district attorney a copy of *The Blade*. "The news story," he said, "is bad enough. That editorial is worse."

Selby glanced at the headlines on the front page.

CARMEN FREELMAN FAINTS WHEN CONFRONTED WITH BILLMEYER'S BODY

Selby's lips clamped together. "Of all the dirty – "

"Read the editorial," Brandon said, indicating a boxed-in editorial on the front page. "Read it aloud, son. I just want to watch your face. It's the one with the headline 'WHO HOLDS THE SACK?' "

Selby read:

"Youth is a splendid thing – in its place. Chivalry is a splendid thing – in its place. But youth and chivalry hardly combine with the responsibilities of a district attorney. The taxpayers of Madison County want results. They want this kept a law-abiding community. It was doubtless a splendid gesture for young, personable, attractive Doug Selby to escort Carmen Freelman out to her automobile, ask her to come back in the morning when she was feeling better, and stand bareheaded at the kerb, letting Gilbert Freelman whisk away the only witness who seems to have any real knowledge of the mysterious circumstances surrounding the death of Desmond Billmeyer. It was a splendid gesture. It would look well in the movies. It would go nicely on the stage. But is it fair to the taxpayers? Is it what a veteran, experienced district attorney would have done under the circumstances?

"Elsewhere in this paper the circumstances are described in detail. Suffice it to say that here was a young, attractive woman who had been intimately associated with Desmond Billmeyer – at least in the conduct of his business. Her employer met his death under circumstances which the county officials freely admit are mysterious. Mrs Gilbert Freelman – or Carmen Freelman as she is known in

Billmeyer's extensive business, and who, so far as is now known, was apparently the last person to see Billmeyer alive – is called in to identify the body and promptly falls in a faint.

"It was the duty of the district attorney to find out why she had fainted. Does District Attorney Selby do so? He does not. He is reported to have taken one arm of Mrs Freelman, while her husband held the other, and gallantly escorted her into an automobile. The machine purred away into the night, with the parties doubtless laughing at the gallant ineptitude of Madison County's district attorney.

"The next act in the drama occurs when Alphonse Baker Carr, veteran of thousands of courtroom battles, very suavely advises District Attorney Selby that Carmen Freelman has employed him – for what reason he doesn't state and apparently wasn't asked – and that she won't be available for questioning.

"And so the handsome young district attorney is left holding the sack.

"Or is it the taxpayers of Madison County who are holding the sack?"

Selby held the paper for a moment, then carefully folded it and placed it on Brandon's desk. "All right," he said, "I led with my chin."

Brandon showed disappointment. "Sometimes I wish I could see you just plain hopping mad. Dammit, I read that and crumpled the dirty sheet up into a ball and threw it across the office. If I'd had hold of the man who wrote that, I'd have wadded the thing into a ball and choked it down his throat."

Selby said, "We're in politics now. We have to take it as well as dish it out."

"Well, let's dish something out then," Brandon said.

"That," Selby announced, "is exactly what I'm going to do. I told you that Gilbert's mother was in to see me."

"Uh huh."

"She let something drop that she didn't intend to. I don't think she knew she was telling me."

"What was it?"

"The way to find Carmen Freelman."

Brandon's eyes glistened. "*Now*, son," he said, "you're really talkin'."

Selby said, "I've a confession to make, Rex. I fell down on the job. The most significant clue of all was in my hands, and I didn't appreciate it, simply because I was taking too much for granted."

"What do you mean?"

Selby said, "Carmen Freelman didn't go to Hollywood and meet Desmond Billmeyer."

"She didn't!" Brandon exclaimed.

Selby shook his head.

"How do you know?"

"The speedometer showed the car had been driven one hundred and fifty-two miles. Sylvia Martin told us about a conversation that was overheard by a man at a filling station where Gilbert stopped to fill up the tank. That was *after* they'd seen the body, *after* Carmen Freelman was supposed to have made her trip to Hollywood and back. When I checked the speedometer, the gas tank was less than half full. If the gasoline tank had been filled up last night, it naturally couldn't have become half empty in driving the three miles out to the Freelman ranch, plus a trip to Orange Heights. The inference is plain: Carmen *didn't* go to Hollywood and the car was driven nearly a hundred and fifty miles *after* Carmen left us Thanksgiving night."

"That's what Gilbert's mother told you?"

"No. What she told me was something different, that Gilbert left about two o'clock with Carmen and didn't get back until after daylight. When he got back, he seemed to have some difficulty hearing things."

"What's that got to do with it?" Brandon asked.

"It means Gilbert had been riding in an airplane. Since private planes are grounded, that means Gilbert took his wife somewhere on a regular passenger plane, and came back alone."

Rex Brandon was reaching for the telephone, even before Selby had finished talking.

CHAPTER TEN

The planed roared through the night. Below lay the dark mystery of the brooding desert. Behind the plane was the fertile belt of citrus land studded with suburban communities which pumped commerce into the life blood of Los Angeles. The transition from rich agricultural land to desert was as abrupt as though some huge knife had cut a dividing line.

In Selby's ears the roar of the motor, reassuringly deepthroated in its steady surge of power, became a soothing lullaby. He felt the strain and tension ooze out of him. His body relaxed to the cushions, and he slept.

It was the sharp dip of the fuselage which wakened him. He saw lights ahead, lights which swung through an arc as the plane banked on one wing tip for a smooth turn over a lighted airport. The throttled-down motor robbed the explosions of their staccato effect and gave place to the singing whine of wind flowing past the streamlined fuselage.

The pilot settled the plane to a smooth landing. Selby, feeling slightly dazed with sleep, emerged to encounter a smiling, courteous young man behind the information desk of a brilliantly lighted office and administration building.

Selby said, "I'd like to rent a car by the hour."

The young man nodded. "The Acme Auto Livery Service makes a special rate to airport customers, and so gets all of our business. It may be difficult getting a car with a driver at this hour, but I can get you a car without a driver with very little delay."

Selby said, "That suits me," and within fifteen minutes found himself behind the wheel of a late model Ford sedan, on the door of which was printed in gilt, "Acme Auto Livery."

Selby began making personal inquiries at each hospital and sanitarium listed in the telephone book, taking in particularly those smaller, private-home affairs.

The fifth that he tried was the Desert Health Cottage Home, and consisted of a central building flanked by two rows of typical screen-covered cottages. Selby was just getting out of his car when he became conscious of a tall, graceful figure emerging from another car parked in the shadows under a shade tree. Selby casually glanced at the figure, then stiffened to attention.

"Good evening, Counsellor," A B Carr said in his peculiarly rich, resonant voice.

Surprised and irritated, Selby stood motionless, watching Carr come toward him. He saw Carr's automobile, a shiny, late model Ford sedan, on the side of which was printed in gilt a neat sign, "Acme Auto Livery."

Carr extended his hand. Selby shook hands. It might have been the casual meeting of two friends.

Carr said, "Do you know, Counsellor, I rather thought you'd be along – as soon as I learned Sheriff Brandon had been telephoning the airplane companies. I don't suppose you'll tell me how you happened to find out she'd gone by plane."

Selby said, "It was the sheriff who did the telephoning?"

"So my informant reported."

"Then you'll have to ask *him* how he found out."

Carr's lips twisted in a smile. "You're an adroit individual, Selby. You *really* are. I don't mind telling you that I don't have half the trouble with any of the big-time city prosecutors I have with you."

"I suppose that's intended as a compliment?"

Carr said, "Come, come, now, Selby. No hard feelings. After all, you know, all's fair in love and war, and, as far as I'm concerned, these little matters are very much like war."

Selby said with dignity, trying to mask his feelings, "I am only trying to interview a witness."

"That's right," Carr said, smiling, "and I am only trying to keep you from interviewing that witness ... However, don't let me detain you. Were we going in?"

"Oh, yes," Selby said, "we're going in."

Side by side they walked up the short stretch of cement walk which communicated with the lighted porch. They passed through the door and into an office, where a young woman glanced up. "Good evening," she said to Carr.

Selby pushed forward. "Do you have a Mrs Gilbert Freelman here?"

"Why, yes," she said. "She's Dr Rapp's patient."

Selby said, "I want to see her."

Carr smiled and shook his head.

Selby said, "I am the district attorney of Madison County. This young woman is an important witness."

The girl behind the desk glanced at Carr, who evidently made some signal behind Selby's back. She said perplexedly, "I'm sorry."

"You mean I can't see her?"

"Orders are to allow absolutely no visitors."

Selby paused for a moment. "What room is she in?" he asked, and, as the young woman hesitated, said, "I've told you who I am. You can conform to what you consider are the doctor's orders if you want to, but you withhold information at your peril."

"She's in cottage twenty-one."

Selby said, "I have here a court order," and fumbled in his pocket; then, with a puzzled frown on his forehead, said, "I must have left it in the car. Excuse me a moment." He started hurriedly for the door, and noticed with satisfaction that Carr remained behind, leaning across the counter and engaging in low-voiced conversation with the young woman behind the desk.

Selby ran down the sidewalk, jumped in his automobile, and backed it up to a point just in front of Carr's machine. Then first making certain the keys were dangling in the ignition lock of Carr's machine, he drove it up to the kerb at exactly the place where he had left his own automobile parked when he had entered the hospital. He switched off the motor, re-entered the hospital, stepped into the telephone booth, closed the soundproof door and called the Acme Auto Livery. "Selby talking," he said. "I rented an automobile from you about an hour ago. Do you have a record of the licence number?"

"Why, yes. Why?"

Selby said, "I parked it, and very foolishly left the keys in the ignition. When I came out to get the car, it wasn't at the place where I'd left it."

"Stolen?"

Selby said, "I don't know. It wasn't there, that's all."

The voice said crisply, "We'll report it to the police immediately. How long ago did you leave the car at the kerb?"

"Just a few minutes," Selby said. "I doubt if the person could have gone more than a block or two."

"Don't worry. We'll pick it up all right. The car has our sign in gilt paint on both sides, and I'll give the licence number to the police."

"Thank you," Selby said, and hung up.

He returned to the desk at the sanitarium and said to the girl, "I wish to talk with the manager."

"I'm very sorry. The manager left word that she wasn't to be disturbed under any circumstances. Perhaps if you could come back tomorrow morning, you – "

Selby said to Carr with every indication of cold rage, "We'll see about this. We'll see what sort of law they have in this town."

"Tut, tut," Carr said. "I've never known you to lose your temper before, Counsellor. You really *must* learn to take these matters calmly. You – "

"We'll damn soon find out what the law is on this point," Selby said angrily.

"You forget that I, too, have had a little experience in legal matters. I think I know my client's rights," Carr said suavely.

Selby stormed out of the door and had the satisfaction of seeing Carr follow along behind him. "Be careful not to violate the speed law, Counsellor," Carr cautioned. "They say it's strictly enforced in this city, particularly in the hospital district. The desert climate, you know, attracts thousands of health seekers, and the city caters to them ... And besides, you can't get away from me. I'll be tagging along behind, so as to present my side of the case at the same time – "

Selby jerked open the door of the automobile he had moved, jumped in, switched on headlights and motor; then, as the engine throbbed to life, slammed the car into gear.

Carr moved with surprising alacrity, his long legs covering the ground back to the shade tree beneath which he had parked his automobile. He jumped in the car that was there, and almost immediately Selby saw headlights flash on in his rear-view mirror.

Selby drove rapidly toward the centre of the business district, then started twisting and turning around corners, as though trying to shake the machine behind him.

Old ABC, manipulating the wheel with deft skill, kept within some thirty-five yards of Selby's bumper. Once, in turning a corner, Selby caught a glimpse of the criminal lawyer's face. He was holding his cigar cocked upward at a rakish angle. His face was wearing a serene smile of complete complacency.

Five minutes later an oncoming car suddenly shot a red spotlight into brilliance. The light shifted from the gilt legend on the side of Selby's car to the licence number; then a moment later the light swung to Old ABC's automobile. Almost instantly Selby heard the low wail of a siren. The district attorney pushed the throttle well down toward the floorboards.

Old ABC hesitated, then poured speed into the car he was driving.

The police car swung into a screaming turn in the middle of the block. The siren was an ear-splitting wail now, but the police machine had lost considerable ground in making the turn. Selby whipped his car around to the left. Old ABC followed, but was unable to quite keep up. At the first sound of the siren Selby had speeded up. It had taken Carr a second or two to make up his mind, and that indecision had cost him distance.

Selby, watching in his rear-view mirror, saw the police car slew around the corner. ABC was giving his automobile everything it had now, but the police car, with its special high-compression head, came roaring alongside. Selby saw Carr shout and gesticulate angrily. The police car crowded him to the kerb. As ABC stopped, Selby swung his car to the right and drove as fast as he dared to the sanitarium, trusting to his official credentials to square any charge of speeding which might be placed against him.

At the sanitarium Selby drove past the administration building, parallel to the line of screened cottages, to a driveway over which a sign bore the words "Ambulance Entrance."

Selby drove in and parked his car.

The cottages had aluminium numbers nailed on the front steps. Selby had no trouble in finding cottage number twenty-one. He tried the door, found it unlocked, and walked into a cosy, screened room. A dim light filtering in from the outside showed bed, table, radio, chaise longue, and two chairs.

A woman's voice said without fear, "I didn't ring. I think you have the wrong cabin."

Selby drew up a chair, sat down, and said, "This is District Attorney Selby, Mrs Freelman. I want to talk with you."

He heard the bedsprings as she drew herself up to stare in the half darkness. He heard her breathe, a swift, rushing intake of startled surprise. But she said nothing.

Selby said, "I just want to tell you a few facts, Mrs Freelman. I know your husband, and I know your husband's father and mother. What's more important, I know something of their backgrounds. I assume you want the love of your husband and the respect of his parents. The only way you can ever keep them is by facing the facts, whatever they are. You can't run away from something you don't want to face without weakening your own character and losing the esteem of those whose esteem means the most to you."

After a few moments she said, "You don't think I'd have been so foolish as to have done anything without telling my husband."

Selby said, "You told him *afterwards*. He's standing back of you, yes. But he'll always remember that you told him afterwards, and not before.

"I don't know how well you know his parents. Charles Freelman came to Madison County years ago and made his way to the top by hard work and self-discipline. You're from the city. When someone asks you about your father-in-law, you say, 'He owns a ranch.' That's what it means to you. It means more than that to a man who's rooted in the soil the way Freelman is. It means that he's carved out a little empire for himself and his family with his two hands. He's done it by steady, patient labour, by shrewd planning. He's making his living, not by juggling finances or out-trading the other man, but by producing it from the ground itself. That does something to a man's character. It makes him straightforward, direct, and very positive of the difference between right and wrong. He may be inarticulate, but don't ever make the mistake of thinking that because he is inarticulate he's dumb.

"Your husband's in love with you – now. He will perhaps stay in love with you. I don't know about that. What's more to the point, you don't know, and he doesn't; but he'll be a lot more proud of you if he can bring you home to the family gatherings as a woman who measures up to the standards of rugged honesty held by his father and his mother.

"I have a car waiting outside. There's a plane due at the airport. You have a very few minutes to make up your mind."

Selby ceased talking. The interval of silence became unduly prolonged. Selby took his pipe from his pocket, filled it with tobacco, heard the bedsprings creak, the sound of rustling motion, then silence.

Selby scratched a match on the sole of his foot.

The light of the match showed him that the bed was empty. Selby reached for the floor lamp.

He heard Carmen Freelman's voice, choked with tears, saying, "Put out that light. I'm dressing."

Sheriff Brandon and Doug Selby sat on one side of the desk, Carmen Freelman on the other. There was no illumination in the room other than the shaded desk lamp which shed a soft green light on the level of the eyes, but flooded the top of the desk with brilliant illumination. The clock – above the glass case in which the sheriff kept weapons that had been used in the perpetration of unusual crimes – said it was twenty minutes past five o'clock.

A knock sounded on the door of the sheriff's outer office.

Brandon strode across the room, unlocked the door, opened it a scant inch, saw that the person in the outer corridor was Gilbert Freelman and pulled back the door. "Come in, Gilbert," he said.

Gilbert Freelman seemed nervous. "You said over the telephone that Carmen was – "

"In here," Selby said.

Carmen pushed back her chair and got to her feet, standing facing her husband with her chin up, her eyes steady, but there was a slight trembling at the corners of her mouth.

Gilbert crossed to her, put his arm around her, held her close to him. "What happened, hon?" he asked.

Selby said, "She decided to come back and give us what assistance she could. She reached that decision of her own free will."

Sheriff Brandon said, "Doug and I thought you should be here before we asked her any questions, Gilbert … Won't you please sit down?"

Gilbert said, "That's awfully damn decent of you folks – after the deal we gave you."

Brandon said, "Forget it."

Selby looked at Carmen Freelman. "Do you want to make a statement now, Mrs Freelman?"

She nodded.

Her husband avoided her eyes. His sensitive features, white and drawn, showed that he was fighting for self-control.

Carmen Freelman said, "I was associated with Mr Billmeyer long enough to get to know the details of his business. For some time I had talked with him about putting up a warehouse of his own, where he could have car unloading facilities and an opportunity to handle truck shipments … You'll understand this may sound entirely irrelevant, but unless I begin at the beginning, I can't explain – "

"Go ahead," Selby said.

Gilbert continued to avoid looking at his wife.

"Mr Billmeyer had two pieces of property. By acquiring a third piece which lay between them, there would have been every opportunity for a warehouse with spur track facilities. Shortly after I was married, my brother-in-law, Stephen, jokingly said to me that he had a piece of property he wanted to sell Mr Billmeyer and asked me the best way to approach him.

"I realized as soon as Stephen began talking about the property that it was the piece Mr Billmeyer had had in mind buying, but I simply told Stephen that the only way to do business with Mr Billmeyer was to beard the lion in his den. I didn't say anything which would lead him to believe that Mr Billmeyer was interested in the property in any way, or that he had any warehouse idea in mind.

"I suppose I have to tell you that Mr Billmeyer was attached to me. He – he had asked me to marry him. I think it was a great shock when I married Gilbert. It made a difference in our business relationship ... I told Mr Billmeyer about Stephen's conversation and told him that Stephen would doubtless approach him. Mr Billmeyer virtually accused me of having tipped Stephen off so that he could make the deal. I indignantly denied this.

"Stephen called on Mr Billmeyer. Mr Billmeyer was an excellent businessman. He managed to convince Stephen that he wasn't interested in the property at all. He even went so far after that as to try to pull the wool over my eyes by telling me he'd decided not to go ahead with the warehouse, and would be interested in selling his two pieces of property if he could get a fair price for them, rather than in buying the intervening piece. That didn't fool me a bit. I knew Mr Billmeyer and knew the way he worked.

"Mr Billmeyer had a close friend, Mr Gillespie. Shortly after this conversation Stephen told Gilbert that he was working on a real estate deal with Gillespie. I had to smile when Gilbert told me, but I didn't say anything, either to Gilbert or to Stephen. I kept Mr Billmeyer's business absolutely to myself. I was, however, anxious for the expiration of the six months' period which I had agreed to remain with the business."

"How did it happen that you agreed to stay on that six months?" Selby asked. "Or, to put it another way, how did it happen that Mr Billmeyer wanted you to?"

She said, "For the simple reason that there were so many details of the business with which I was familiar, details about which Mr Billmeyer knew nothing. He said he had to break in someone else to take my place."

"I see. Go ahead."

She hesitated for a moment, then said, "I didn't realize just what he had in mind, or I never would have agreed to stay on for the six months … About a week ago Mr Billmeyer wanted me to – to leave Gilbert and go away with him. He offered me everything, a partnership in the business, an independent income, anything that I wanted. When I refused, he began to brood. I became concerned about him, and then on Wednesday he started to drink. It was the first time I had known him to touch a drop.

"There was something in Mr Billmeyer's past that had something to do with liquor. I don't know just what it was, but he had a horror of touching it. He wouldn't ever take a drop … Then Wednesday afternoon I smelled liquor on his breath and became apprehensive. I didn't like the way he looked at me. He kept following me with his eyes, saying nothing, but always staring. However, nothing happened, and nothing was said. I left the office Wednesday night. Mr Billmeyer was still there.

"On Thanksgiving, about three o'clock, Mr Billmeyer called me on the telephone. He said that something had happened which had greatly shocked him, that he couldn't explain over the telephone. He wanted to know if I would meet him at six o'clock."

"In Hollywood?" Selby asked, glancing significantly at Rex Brandon.

"No. Las Alidas."

"*Where*?"

"In Las Alidas. In front of the Las Alidas Hotel. He asked me to leave the house before four, saying I was going to Hollywood; but to go to Las Alidas and wait for him."

Selby tried to keep surprise from his face. "You met him there?"

"Yes."

"Was he wearing that tweed suit?"

"No. He was wearing a double-breasted checkered suit."

"Was he driving a car?"

"Yes."

"Did you see the car?"

"No, I didn't. I saw the headlights come up behind me, and then the lights switched on and Mr Billmeyer walked along the sidewalk, opened the door of my car, and slid into the seat beside me."

"Had he been drinking?"

"There was liquor on his breath, yes, but he seemed – Well, he didn't seem intoxicated."

"Were you frightened?" Selby asked.

She said, "Not until after I got there; then I began to worry a bit. But I'd told Mr Billmeyer I'd be there, and I wasn't going to let him down."

"Go ahead," Selby said.

"Well, Mr Billmeyer made a most extraordinary request. He – he wanted to know if I'd give him an alibi."

"What!" Selby exclaimed.

She said, "That's just what he said, an alibi."

"For what?"

"He didn't say. He said something had happened which would change his entire life. He seemed very nervous and – well, shaken. He wanted to know if I would tell my family, particularly Stephen, that I had gone into Hollywood, had met him at the Hollywood office."

"Then what happened?"

"Mr Billmeyer said, 'You may return home about eleven-thirty. If anyone asks you for details, you're too tired to talk. Pretend to be annoyed with me, but simply say that you went in to see me at the office and that after you found the paper I wanted, there was some business we had to discuss'."

"Then what?"

"Then he got out of the automobile and stood at the kerb smiling at me. He seemed more relieved and more natural than I'd seen him ever since my marriage. I parked the car, went to a movie, stayed until that show ended, went to another movie, left in time to get back about eleven-forty-five ... And that's all I know."

"Why didn't you tell us this when we asked you to identify the body?" Sheriff Brandon asked.

She said, "If you'll remember, Sheriff, you didn't give me any intimation that it was Mr Billmeyer. You simply took me over to see the body. When I saw who it was, I – well, I fainted, that's all. When I came to, I really didn't feel able to discuss the matter. I intended to in the morning ... Then, on the way home, I told Gilbert, and Gilbert pointed out several things that hadn't occurred to me. I had made what amounted to a rendezvous with my employer without the knowledge of my husband. I hadn't gone to Hollywood, after telling the family I had. I told Gilbert about going to the movies. Gilbert believed me. He wasn't certain whether others would ... He thought it might be better if things could be arranged so I didn't have to tell my story. He called up Mr Carr and asked Carr what to do, told him about what had happened to Mr Billmeyer. Mr Carr said for us to come up there and – Well, you know the rest."

"How much did you tell Carr?"

"Everything – the whole story. He insisted on all the details, wanted to know all about Mr Billmeyer, about the real estate deal, and everything. Mr Billmeyer was dead, so there was no need to keep the business affairs secret. Mr Carr impressed upon me that, as my lawyer, he had to know everything. I told him."

For a long minute there was silence in the sheriff's office; then Selby said, "Mrs Freelman, I think there's only one thing for you to do. Give this story the widest publicity, every detail of it. Emphasize the fact there was something Mr Billmeyer asked you in connection with a real estate transaction, and that you were placed in the embarrassing position of having your brother-in-law acting as agent for the sale of the property without knowing the real identity of the purchaser."

"But how will I explain that – that running away?"

"You won't," Selby said. "You were in a state of collapse. The doctor ordered you to a sanitarium. As soon as you felt sufficiently rested to talk, you returned here *of your own volition*."

She said, "But you did some clever detective work finding out where I was and – "

"That doesn't need to enter it," Selby said. "So far as I am concerned, no one will ever know that I went to the sanitarium and brought you back."

Her eyes widened. "Why," she exclaimed in surprise, "you mean you're not going to give out the story about finding me? It was a clever piece of detective work. It – "

Selby said, "I didn't find you. You returned of your own volition."

The legs of Gilbert Freelman's chair scraped along the floor as he suddenly got to his feet. His hand shot across the desk, gripped Selby's hand. "I don't suppose," he said, "you have any idea what this means to me. I realize now how wrong it was for Carmen to run away. It had to come out sooner or later, and I know now that if we'd handled it the other way – " His voice choked up.

Sheriff Brandon said, "Forget it, son. You made a mistake, but it's all right."

For a moment Gilbert Freelman's eyes were trying to say the things that his lips couldn't express. Then he turned to Carmen. He opened his arms and, as she came to him, gently, tenderly drew her close.

CHAPTER ELEVEN

Sylvia Martin was waiting for Selby when the district attorney entered his office late Saturday morning.

"Hello, sleepy. Had breakfast?"

Selby said, "Confidentially, and strictly between us, the answer is no."

She laughed. "Don't you suppose we could run out for a bite of breakfast – and anyone who saw us would think we were having an early lunch?"

"We might try," Selby said. "I want to look through the mail."

Sylvia said, "Boy, oh boy, was that a story to slap in *The Blade's* face in this morning's paper! Of course, Doug, it's swell for the readers, but just between you and me, how did she happen to come back?"

Selby said, "She felt sufficiently recovered from her nervousness to face the ordeal."

"With perhaps a little detective work on the part of the district attorney?"

"I wouldn't know – not for publication anyway." Sylvia said, "I've lost a job."

"How come?"

"I was selling this story to the Los Angeles papers. It got so hot they're sending their own reporters down ... You know, Doug, I'm wondering if the Los Angeles papers will be as – well, as charitable to Carmen Freelman as we were."

Selby said, "I don't think it makes so much difference now. First impressions with anything like that are what count … There's one thing about her story that bothers me."

"What?"

"From what Gilbert's mother said, the first telephone call, the one that seemed to upset her so much, came just as they were sitting down to dinner, about ten minutes after two; then another call came for her about three. It was the first call that upset her so terribly. The three o'clock call was Billmeyer's."

"You think she's holding something back, Doug?"

"I keep wondering where her brother enters the picture."

"Probably Carr dug him up to use as a point of contact to make it seem that Carmen had been taken away as – well, sort of a family affair."

Selby said, "Carr's a deep one."

The door opened, and Rex Brandon thrust his head in. "Busy?"

"Come on in, Rex," Selby invited. "I only woke up about half an hour ago. I haven't had breakfast. Sylvia and I were debating whether we could talk better over coffee and ham and eggs."

Brandon said, "Suppose I telephone the Missus and we all go out to my place for a little snack, and – "

The telephone rang.

Selby picked up the instrument, said, "Hello," and a woman's voice said, "This is Inez, Doug. I want to see you right away on an important matter. I – I have someone with me."

Selby hesitated. "I have a very important appointment in about fifteen minutes."

"Can't I possibly see you before then, Doug?"

"Could you come up right away?"

"Yes."

"Come on."

Selby dropped the receiver and said, "Inez Stapleton seems all worked up about something. Go ahead and telephone your wife,

Rex. I'll be through with her in a few minutes and join you at your house."

"Okay," Brandon said, grinning down at Sylvia. "Come on, sister. Whatever Inez is going to tell him she won't want to discuss in the presence of a representative of *The Clarion*."

Sylvia said, "Don't let her keep you, Doug. My own stomach is telegraphing complaints to the commissary department. Working on a morning paper and getting to bed in the wee small hours makes breakfast a big event in my day."

"If it takes longer than fifteen minutes," Selby said, "I'll declare a recess."

They had been gone about two minutes when Amorette Standish appeared in the door to announce Inez Stapleton. "There's a woman with her," she said, "but Inez wants to talk with you for a moment first."

Selby said, "Send her in."

Amorette quietly nodded and withdrew. A moment later Inez Stapleton entered, tall, slim, and with that assurance which is so frequently associated with wealth and breeding.

When Inez Stapleton's father had lived in Madison City, he had been one of the city's most powerful men. In the carefree days when Doug was a young attorney with more leisure than clients, he and Inez had been seen frequently together. Then, as they had drifted apart after Selby's election, Inez had been admitted to the bar, and very frankly challenged Doug to *try* and forget her, promising to be a thorn in his flesh.

"Hello, Counsellor," she said, her large, dark eyes softening as she smiled.

"Good morning to you, Counsellor," Selby retorted. "Are you being a thorn in my flesh this morning, or is this purely a social call?"

"This morning I'm a thorn."

"Sit down and tell me about it. Who's with you?"

"A client."

"To the client," Selby said, taking out his watch with a businesslike air, "I have an important appointment in fifteen minutes. To you, confidentially, privately and personally, I'm going to confess that it's a breakfast date. I was up nearly all Thursday night, got to bed about four o'clock this morning. I only dropped in at the office to look over the mail and see what was new before keeping a breakfast date with the sheriff."

"How's your before-breakfast disposition, Doug?"

"Savage."

"Perhaps," she said, somewhat wistfully, "it's just as well you remain a bachelor."

"Perhaps it's my disposition that keeps me a bachelor."

"Oh, I don't know … However, we didn't come here to discuss your matrimonial prospects … Doug, I have Mrs Grines with me. She's my client."

"You mean Mrs Pervis Grines?" Selby asked, showing his surprise.

"No. Mrs *Carleton* Grines."

"What," Selby demanded, "do you know about Carleton Grines?"

"A good deal. I want you to listen to what my client has to say, Doug. I want you to get the story directly from her. I think it'll mean more to you if you hear it that way than if you get it second hand."

"Bring her in," Selby said.

"I'll get her," Inez told him. "You wait here."

The woman Inez Stapleton escorted into the room was entirely different from the type Selby had expected to see. Here was no flashy, assertive woman of the type one would have associated with the Carleton Grines who had left Oklahoma in disgrace, only to wind up in an Oregon jail. She was quiet in appearance to the point of being demure. Her face was sensitive and alert.

"Mrs Carleton Grines," Inez Stapleton introduced.

"Won't you be seated?" Selby invited, and added apologetically, "I have only a very few minutes. Therefore, I'd prefer to get a preliminary outline now and fill in details at a subsequent interview."

Inez Stapleton smiled. "I think that you'll find Mrs Grines can handle the matter very concisely, Doug." She turned to her client. "You understand what the district attorney wants. Please give him the highlights of the story as you have told it to me."

Mrs Grines turned steady, dark brown eyes to the district attorney. "I first met Carleton in Oklahoma. I never met any of his family. He was in trouble there several times. He was likable but headstrong, and he was given to liquor. It was his one fault. I was fascinated by his daring, his quick wit, his devil-may-care manner. He was ten years older than I, and he turned my head completely."

She paused and turned to Inez Stapleton. "This is the part you wanted me to tell?"

"Go right ahead," Inez said.

Mrs Grines spoke in a well-modulated voice which showed evidences of culture. Her eyes were expressive and intelligent. Quite apparently she had the ability of letting her thoughts flow without conscious effort into words, while her attention was left free to watch the reactions of the district attorney.

"We left Oklahoma the first of November, 1931. We went to Arizona. We were married there. We used fictitious names because Carleton didn't want his brother to know of his marriage, and didn't want to do anything which would attract the attention of the authorities to him. At the time he left Oklahoma, it hadn't been decided whether they would bring him back to face additional charges."

Inez Stapleton nodded for her client to proceed.

"We went to Oregon. Within a week Carleton had a job. He was smart and he made a good impression. He promised me he'd never touch another drop of liquor as long as he lived.

Foolishly, I believed him … Carleton made a down payment on a secondhand car. He said he needed it to go back and forth to work. On Thanksgiving day, 1931, he started drinking. There was an accident, and when the officers picked him up, they checked back on his record and found out about the trouble he'd had in Oklahoma. That settled it. As Carleton expressed it, they threw the book at him … There was a jail break. Carleton, wild and reckless, was in on it up to his neck. The ringleader protected the few who escaped by at first refusing to give their names. Later on some of the men were captured and gave the officers the names of the others who had escaped. Then the ringleader 'confessed.' That was all so much eyewash.

"What actually happened, the convicts had got together and given the officers the names of the men who had got entirely free as being those who had died in the fire. I didn't know that until an anonymous voice on the telephone told me that if I'd go to California and call on Mr Desmond Billmeyer I'd find out something which would be very much to my advantage. I called on him. He didn't recognize me. He was, of course, wealthy. He said he had no recollection of his prior life."

Selby, keenly interested and utterly oblivious of the passing of time now, asked, "Did you tell him about his past life?"

"Yes. I could see that it gave him a terrific jolt."

"When was this?"

"Last Tuesday."

"And what was the final outcome of the interview?"

"Carleton was fair about it. He said that he couldn't remember me, that he certainly couldn't say that I was his wife; nor, he confessed, could he say that I was not his wife. He said that he couldn't remember the early part of his life, that he hadn't known what his name was … Evidently, he'd been injured in that fire. He said the only thing to do was to investigate my story. If it were true, he'd make some sort of a financial adjustment, but could hardly be expected to pick up the thread of a life where it had been broken ten years ago."

"What did you say to that?"

"It seemed fair. After all, Mr Selby, ten years is a long time."

"Meaning that you have other interests?"

"Not at this particular moment, but – well, I have had."

"Did Carleton get in touch with his brother?" Selby asked.

"I think he found out that Pervis was in Las Alidas. I think that Carleton was on his way to see this brother in Las Alidas. I think he intended to walk in and surprise him."

Selby said, "Do you mean that he wanted to put on old clothes, pretend that the world hadn't been any too good to him, and then surprise his brother by disclosing his affluence and his true identity?"

"Something like that … From what I've learned later, there was some oil property. Carleton's brother couldn't touch it until after a certain number of years when Carleton's death could have been established by law. Perhaps Carleton's brother – Oh, I don't know … Miss Stapleton said you should know the facts."

Selby said, "I want to think this over."

Inez Stapleton, crisply businesslike, said, "I think that's all, Mrs Grines. We've given Mr Selby the highlights. You can, of course, get the details and proof at any time you want, Doug. You might step outside now, Mrs Grines."

"What," Selby asked, "are you going to do, Inez?"

She said, "Naturally, I'm going to establish my client as the surviving widow. *The Blade's* running the full story tonight. I thought you should know it in advance."

"Thanks," Selby said, moving with her to the door.

For two or three seconds Inez stood looking into his eyes, apparently trying to find some words with which she could express her thoughts; then abruptly her lips tightened, and she said, "I won't keep you any longer from your breakfast conference, Doug."

And something in the way she said it made Selby realize she knew Sylvia Martin was to be at that conference.

Chapter Twelve

The sky was clouding up. Low, rain-sodden clouds were drifting in from the southeast, cutting down the light and making Sheriff Brandon's dining-room seem filled with shadows.

Mrs Brandon brought in a steaming plate of muffins, placed them next to the platter of ham and eggs, and looked around over the table. "You folks got everything you want?" she asked.

Selby looked up from his cup filled with golden brown coffee mixed with rich cream. "My stomach," he said, "is as contented as a purring cat in front of a fireplace."

Mrs Brandon drew up a chair and sat down. "Well, I may as well have a cup of coffee," she said, "and a muffin ... Oh, all right, Rex, give me a piece of that ham. Seems like we had breakfast only about an hour ago, but, sakes alive, a little good food isn't going to hurt a body ... Now then, Saturday afternoon is a legal holiday, and you folks are just going to stay here and rest up. You've been dashing around too much, all of you."

Selby laughed. "This morning wasn't a legal holiday, and I was hardly in my office at all."

"Well, you certainly worked enough at night ... Rex, what time *did* you get in this morning?"

Brandon grinned and said, "I took my shoes off and sneaked in, Ma."

Mrs Brandon placed a generous slab of butter on the interior of a muffin, poured thick, yellow cream from a pitcher into her coffee, and stirred in two heaping teaspoonfuls of sugar. "Well, I

101

suppose you're goin' to talk about murders now. Sakes alive, ruin good food talkin' about people killing other people … Well, go ahead. What's new?"

Brandon winked. "She's dying with curiosity, Doug, and tries to mask it; but if something happened and we *didn't* talk about the murder case, she'd feel she'd been short-changed."

Selby said, "I've been saving a little information I got from Inez Stapleton just before I left the office."

Mrs Brandon said, "You watch out for that girl, Doug Selby. She's in love with you."

Sylvia Martin said, "It's all right for you to warn Doug against these other women, but don't you dare say anything against *me*."

Mrs Brandon looked at Sylvia over the top of her glasses. "Wouldn't hurt *you* none to get married and settle down," she said. "What'd Inez Stapleton say, Doug?"

Brandon said, "See? What'd I tell you? She's just dying to find out about that murder."

Selby said, "I think Inez has got in on a pretty good case." He then went on to relate the conversation he'd had with Inez and her client.

When he had finished, Sylvia Martin said bitterly, "She would have to release that so *The Blade* would have the story this evening. Don't think for a minute she'd ever give *me* a break on a news story."

Sheriff Brandon said jokingly, "That's all right, Sylvia. We'll let you come out tomorrow with a solution on the whole case."

Sylvia made a point of ostentatiously whipping a pencil and notepaper from her purse. "That's a promise," she said. "Go ahead, gentlemen. Let's have the solution."

Brandon said, "If it wasn't for Doc Trueman and his report on the cause of death, we wouldn't have anything to worry about. It all fits into a perfect picture."

Selby said, "Somehow, I have an idea we're overlooking the important clue in this case."

"What?" Sylvia asked.

Selby said, "If I knew what it was, I wouldn't be overlooking it. I'm not certain but what it may be that suit of clothes. Where did Billmeyer get them?"

"Some place where they'd been carefully kept for ten years," Sylvia said thoughtfully.

Brandon gave that statement consideration. "Probably, Doug, he'd saved those clothes as the one clue which linked him up with his past. The man may have lost his memory, but he didn't lose his clothes, and he thought the clothes might give him a clue to his real identity."

Selby nodded. "I've thought of that, but there's the envelope that was in the inside pocket. That envelope was addressed to Grines at General Delivery, Phoenix, and had the return address of Cherokee Flats, Oklahoma. If Billmeyer suddenly found himself robbed of his identity, and wondering what his name was, be had only to look in the inside pocket of his suit and find that envelope. That would have told him enough so he'd have made inquiries in Cherokee Flats."

Brandon frowned. "That's right."

Selby went on, "His wife would have been more apt to have preserved that suit than anyone. Apparently Billmeyer had no contact with his past life until last Tuesday. According to the wife's statement, she brought up his past life. It is, therefore, quite probable that she produced that tweed suit he was wearing at the time of his death. It would have proved her claim that she was his wife."

"But what would have been her motive in killing him?" Brandon asked.

"That," Selby said, "is the part that really fits. Until Tuesday, Billmeyer didn't know he was married. Then his wife shows up. He realizes then that he was married, and that if anything should happen to him, she would inherit all of his property. Probably that didn't suit his ideas. He *may* have wanted to leave his business to Carmen Freelman. He intended to make a will. If he died before he made the will, his wife profited.

"Then there's the brother. He had been counting on stepping into a lot of property as soon as the statutory time ran for the law to presume his brother was dead. He had only a short time to wait. Then the bad penny turns up – a brother whom he had always considered a financial liability, a worthless member of the family who was better off dead … Obviously, the temptation was strong."

Sylvia said, "You have two suspects. Both of them sound equally good to me."

Selby said, "That means there's some clue we're overlooking; either that, or that we aren't correctly interpreting the facts."

Selby, who had been raising his coffee cup, suddenly lowered it to his saucer.

Sylvia Martin, watching Selby's expression, said, "What is it, Doug?"

By way of answer, Selby pushed back his chair, went to the telephone and called J C Gillespie's number. "Mr Gillespie?" he asked when he heard a voice on the line.

"Yes."

"This is District Attorney Selby."

"Oh, good morning, Mr Selby – or is it good afternoon?"

Selby laughed. "It's almost on the dividing line. There's a question I want to ask you."

"What is it?"

"Did you see Stephen Freelman on Friday?"

"No."

"Have you heard from him since the visit he paid you on Thanksgiving?"

"No, I haven't … Of course, you understand, under the circumstances, Mr Selby, I wouldn't have anything to tell him.

I'd have to confess to him that I was acting as – well, as a dummy."

"I understand," Selby said. "I was just trying to check up, that's all."

"Nothing else I can do for you?"

"No, thank you."

Selby hung up and walked over to stand at the table with his hands resting on the back of the chair, frowning meditatively down at Rex Brandon. "That, Rex," he said, "is the most significant piece of information in the whole case."

"What?"

"That Stephen Freelman *didn't* get in touch with Gillespie on Friday."

"Why?"

"Don't you see?" Selby said. "It must mean Stephen knew there was no use. He realized that in dealing with Gillespie he was dealing with a dummy for Desmond Billmeyer. Now then, *how* did he get that information?"

Brandon thought for a moment, then abruptly wiped his lips, pushed his plate back, and got up. "Wanta go now, Doug?" he asked.

Selby said simply, "Yes."

The Freelman family was at lunch when Selby and Brandon dropped in. "I'm sorry," Selby apologized, "for interrupting your lunch, but there are some things I want to know."

Stephen said, "Come on in and sit down. Or have you had lunch?"

Brandon said, "We've eaten, thanks."

Stephen, noticing the official gravity of their faces, said, "Well, how about it, boys? Do you want to take us one at a time, put us under a bright light, and give us a third degree?"

Selby said, "I can ask the questions anywhere, but perhaps some of you would prefer to answer them privately."

Stephen said hastily, "Well now, that's a good idea." He laughed boisterously. "I'll answer *my* questions in private. The rest of you can answer right here."

There were a few smiles around the table.

Corliss Ditmer suddenly interposed to say, "Aren't we all acting like a bunch of ninnies on this case? Doug Selby and Rex Brandon are square shooters. Personally, I'm not satisfied we're giving them a square deal."

Her eyes moved around the table, came to rest for a moment on Carmen, who flushed under her make-up.

Stephen said, "Nonsense, Corliss. We're doing everything we can. Didn't Carmen come back of her own accord and – "

Corliss stared at him steadily. "Do *you*," she asked, "believe that?"

Stephen hastily lit a cigarette.

Charles Freelman said gravely, "Sit down, boys. I guess I'm still the head of this family. There's not going to be any holding out. What do you want to know?"

Selby and Brandon accepted the chairs Charles Freelman drew up. Selby said, "There are two things I want to get straight … Stephen, you were trying to sell Gillespie a piece of property, weren't you?"

"Yes."

Selby met his eyes squarely. "You knew that Gillespie was a dummy for Billmeyer. How did you know?"

Stephen hastily raised the cigarette to his lips, took a deep drag, looked around the table, seemed painfully conscious of the eyes of the others on him, of the silence which magnified Carmen's quick gasp.

"I don't know what makes you think I knew anything of the sort," Stephen said, and his attempt at defiance made him seem very much on the defensive.

Selby said, "It's so obvious that I should have thought of it a long time ago. You were very anxious to see Gillespie on

Thursday. He was going to give you a final answer on Friday. Yet you didn't go near him on Friday, and you haven't been near him since. That means you knew. Now, *how* did you know?"

Stephen tapped ashes from the end of his, cigarette. His left hand crumpled his napkin. "To tell you the truth," he said, "I – well, I wasn't quite as simple as Billmeyer thought I was. I thought he was playing me along. I got a friend in the real estate business to ring him up and make him an offer on one of the adjoining pieces of property he held. The offer was for about twice what it was worth. Of course, if Billmeyer had accepted, my man would have said it was only a tentative offer and backed down. The point was, Billmeyer told him the property wasn't for sale. Then when Gillespie started negotiating, I knew what was happening."

Selby said, "There was something else. That might have given you a clue, but you'd certainly have gone to see Gillespie on Friday if you hadn't *known*."

Stephen said, "Well, to tell you the truth, my hearing has always been extraordinarily acute. While I was talking with Gillespie, he went into another room. I – well, I heard him put through a call to Billmeyer."

"That's better," Selby said. "Now what did you do after you left Gillespie on Thanksgiving? Did you go to look over the property?"

"No," Stephen said, "I didn't. I knew he was stalling. I needed that commission – badly. I knew Gillespie was acting for Billmeyer. I knew that Billmeyer had called Carmen to go in to the office in Hollywood. I thought it was about this deal … I made up my mind that I'd go to Billmeyer direct and tell him to quit beating around the bush, that we'd get the cards on the table, and I'd find out definitely where I stood."

"What did you do?" Selby asked. "Where did you go?"

Stephen glanced around the table as though seeking encouragement from the other members of the family, and found none.

"I went to Hollywood – to the office," he blurted. "The office was dark. The janitor told me Billmeyer hadn't been in all day. I asked if Carmen Freelman had been in. He said she hadn't … There you are. I – well, you can realize how I felt – under the circumstances. Carmen was my brother's wife."

Selby turned to Carmen. "Now then," he said, "it's your turn."

Her face showed surprise. "Why, I – I've told you everything."

"When you called A B Carr to act as your attorney, did the suggestion come from you or your husband?"

She hesitated for just the fraction of a second, then said, "It came from me."

"I'd like to know a little more about that."

Gilbert leaned forward in his chair. "Well, I can answer that. We went to Carr's house. We told him the story. Carr said that a physician should see Carmen so that he could sign a certificate. He called Dr Lewis A Rapp. He met us at the airport. He looked at Carmen, asked her a couple of questions, listened to her heart with a stethoscope, looked at the pupils of her eyes, tapped her knees for reflexes, and told Carr that she must have absolute rest. He suggested that she go to a sanitarium where she wouldn't be disturbed."

"Who else was present?" Selby asked.

"No one."

"Your brother wasn't there?" Selby asked Carmen.

She shook her head.

"How did it happen Carr had your brother with him when he called at my office?"

Gilbert said, "And I can answer *that*. Carr told me on the way back in the plane, just before we landed, that he thought it would be a good plan to have Carmen's brother with him when he called on you, and let it appear that his connection was through Milton instead of through either Carmen or me."

"How," Selby asked, "did he know Carmen had a brother?"

"Why, I – I guess we must have said something about it."

"He didn't ask you where he could get in touch with Milton or for Milton's address?"

"No."

Selby said, "When Carr called on me, he had Milton Gregory with him. He seemed unusually concerned about letting Milton do any of the talking. He hardly let the boy open his mouth. In other words, he was afraid that if I began talking with Milton, I'd find out something. Now, Milton didn't know anything to tell me. He didn't know where his sister was, unless Carr had told him; and Carr certainly wouldn't have been foolish enough to have done that – not under the circumstances."

Carmen's eyes were on the tablecloth.

Selby said, "The question arises, therefore, *what was it Milton Gregory knew which Carr was afraid I'd find out if Milton did any talking?*"

"It would seem," Selby went on, after the interval of silence which followed his last question had become strained, "that Carr had already been in contact with Milton Gregory, knew of him, and that Carmen knew all about that. Therefore, when a suggestion was made that she should see a lawyer, Carmen promptly thought of A B Carr."

Again there was silence; then Gilbert said, "Well, does it make any difference? Suppose Milton *had* been in to see Carr? What does that have to do with this case?"

"That," Selby said doggedly, "is what I propose to find out. The telephone call which upset your wife was received shortly after two o'clock on Thanksgiving. The telephone call which came from Desmond Billmeyer was about three o'clock. No one has claimed Billmeyer called twice."

Carmen abruptly looked up to meet Selby's eyes. "I'm not going to answer any questions about that." Her voice rose, and became almost hysterical. "Do you understand, Mr Selby? Not a question."

Charles Freelman said, "I'm sorry, Selby, but that seems to be the answer. I wish Carmen hadn't taken that attitude, but," he added, his jaw squaring doggedly, "Carmen is a Freelman, and us Freelmans hang together. We're sort of standing back of her."

Quick tears came to Carmen's eyes.

Selby said, "Would you go so far as to tell me that Milton's business with Carr had nothing to do with Billmeyer, either directly or indirectly?"

She said, "I c-c-can't, Mr Selby. I can't s-s-say a thing about it."

Selby said, "There are ways of finding out. There are easy ways and hard ways. If you'd tell me the truth, it might be the easy way. If I can't get it the easy way, then I'll have to get it the hard way."

They waited for her to answer then, but she only shook her head.

Charlie Freelman got up to his feet. "That's it, boys. You've got to get it the hard way."

CHAPTER THIRTEEN

Rain which had started as a drizzle about two o'clock Saturday afternoon gathered intensity and had become a steady downpour by five. Pelting against the windows of the sheriff's office, the rain formed rivulets which zigzagged irregularly down off the glass. Aside from the lights in the sheriff's office, the courthouse was dark and silent.

Selby and the sheriff sat at the sheriff's battered desk, waiting for important telephone calls. For the most part they were silent. Selby, puffing thoughtfully at his pipe, was thinking out various angles of the case, and Brandon, with deep respect for Selby's powers of analysis, spoke only in answer to such comments as Selby made from time to time.

The telephone rang. Brandon answered it, listened for several seconds, said, "Okay, keep on working on it. If you get anything let me know."

He hung up, said to Selby, "The Los Angeles police. Milton Gregory has disappeared. Can't get a trace of him anywhere."

Selby nodded, kept on smoking without comment.

After an interval of ten minutes the telephone rang again. Brandon said, "Sheriff's office. Yes ... Who ... Oh, yes – yes, this is Sheriff Brandon himself ... What's that? Oh, yes, Mr Rochester of the Sears National Bank. Yes, Mr Rochester, what is it?"

There was an interval during which the message coming in over the telephone caused Brandon's face to show surprise; then he said, "Thank you. I'll keep it confidential – as much as possible ... Yes, that's all right ... Goodbye."

He hung up the telephone, turned to Selby. "Man by the name of Rochester at the Sears National. Billmeyer had an account there. He doesn't think they handled any of Billmeyer's business. He says that Billmeyer telephoned him on Wednesday morning and said that he'd want thirty-five thousand dollars in cash to use as an initial payment on a real estate deal he intended to close sometime Thanksgiving afternoon or evening. He said he wanted to have the money ready to put into an escrow, and that there were certain reasons why he couldn't use a cheque."

"And he got the money?" Selby asked.

"He got the money, thirty-five one-thousand-dollar bills. The banker says he took the precaution of taking the numbers and that he's sending a copy of that list by special messenger with instructions to deliver it here to my office at the courthouse. He – "

There was a knock at the door. Brandon frowned at the interruption; then as he hesitated about going to the door, he heard Sylvia Martin's cheery, "*Hoo-hoo!* How about letting me in?"

Brandon, grinning, opened the door.

"Brought you folks the latest paper," Sylvia said. "The evening *Blade* hot off the press, hot under the collar, and bitter against the county officials ... Are you talking privately, or would it be all right for an enterprising reporter to horn in?"

"An enterprising reporter," Brandon said, "could horn in ... Gosh, it must be raining hard outside."

"It certainly is," Sylvia said, slipping out of her dripping raincoat and placing her umbrella in the rack near the door. "Coming down cats and dogs."

Brandon looked at *The Blade* which had big headlines.

WIDOW CLAIMS BILLMEYER ESTATE, ADMITS

HUSBAND FUGITIVE FROM JUSTICE
SHERIFF AND DA COMPLETELY BAFFLED

Sylvia indicated the paper. "They certainly do fight dirty," she said. "My boss sent me up to get an interview so he could deliver a proper editorial roast. Do I get it now or later?"

"What," Selby asked, "do you want?"

"Some peg on which I can hang a news story, and on the news story the boss can write an editorial."

Brandon said, "We're making progress but we don't have anything definite."

Sylvia's eyes were pleading. "Haven't you," she asked, "got a thing?"

"Nothing you can use," Selby said.

"I've got some bad news for you. I was hoping you'd have something to offset it."

"What's the bad news?" Brandon asked.

"One of the big Los Angeles dailies has sent its ace reporter, Joseph Bagley Raft, down to cover the case. Raft is the man who cracked the Borden murder mystery, who got the confession in the Howlitt case. He's resourceful and ingenious, and he doesn't care how he gets the news, just so he gets it. He's made the crack that his paper is going to publish a complete solution of the case by Tuesday at the latest, and that after that all you'll have to do will be to go out and make the arrest."

"Talk," Brandon said, "is cheap."

"Not Joe Raft's talk," Sylvia said. "When he talks, people listen, and when he puts the words on paper, he gets money."

Brandon said, "Then he must have unearthed some clue we don't know anything about."

"Or," Selby supplemented, "discovered the significance of some clue we have, but which we haven't appreciated."

"What could that be?" Sylvia Martin asked.

"It might be the suit of clothes."

"You mean that tweed suit Billmeyer was wearing?"

"Yes."

Brandon said, "It was a suit he'd had ten years ago. He lost his memory at that time. About the only thing that suit indicates is that shortly before he died he recovered his memory."

Selby narrowed his eyes thoughtfully. "Go ahead, Rex, keep on talking. I think you're getting ready to say something."

Brandon looked at him in surprise. "There's nothing new in that line of reasoning, Doug. That's the way we had it figured all along."

"I know it is," Selby said. "We got that far and then stopped. I think we've been on the right track all along, but we haven't followed that track far enough. We stopped at the crucial point."

"Well," Brandon said, "he went and got his old suit of clothes. Now that probably means he'd forgotten all about being Billmeyer – although I suppose that his memory *could* have come back to him so that he'd have remembered the Billmeyer part and the other part, too."

Selby said, "That's the part that doesn't check, Rex. He suddenly remembered all about being Carleton Grines. He went and got that suit of clothes, and put it on ... Now *why* would he have done that – if he remembered the Billmeyer part?"

Brandon thought that over for a moment, then nodded. "You're right, son. The fact that he got *that* suit of clothes shows that he had forgotten all about being Billmeyer. He remembered only that he was Carleton Grines. That intervening ten years was a blank to him, and the probabilities are he didn't know how many years it had been – thought it was perhaps just yesterday that his mind had slipped."

"That's it," Sylvia Martin exclaimed eagerly. "That must be it! He found himself wearing someone else's clothes, and because he knew he'd escaped from jail and that he was wanted by the police, he was afraid he'd stolen the clothes. He went to the place where he'd left his old suit. The suit was still there and he got into it, although it was pretty tight – "

"Now we're getting some place," Brandon said. "That suit was tight. That convinced him he hadn't been wearing it for some time. That must have put him wise to the fact that his lapse of memory had covered a considerable period of time."

Selby, pushing his hands down deep in his pockets, said, "There's something else about that suit that's significant."

"What?"

"Not in connection with the suit itself, but in connection with the other one."

"What other one?" Brandon asked.

"The one he was wearing at the time he recovered his memory."

"I don't get you, son."

Selby said, "If our information is correct and Billmeyer drew thirty-five thousand dollars out of the bank and was carrying that on his person when Billmeyer suddenly vanished into thin air and Carleton Grines took his place, you can see what happened. Grines found himself very much a fugitive from justice wearing the clothes of some strange man, *and in the pockets of those clothes were thirty-five one-thousand-dollar bills.*"

The springs on Brandon's swivel chair creaked as the sheriff sat up straight. "By George! The thing must have happened just that way. He found the thirty-five thousand dollars. Naturally, he thought he'd been guilty of some crime that had paid off big, and – and – "

"And," Selby finished, "he wanted to find out what that crime was, how serious it was, whether it was murder or robbery, or perhaps kidnapping. So what did he do? He did something that would tell him about what he'd done to get thirty-five thousand dollars."

"And that something," Brandon said, "took him to Orange Heights."

The three of them exchanged glances. It was Sylvia Martin who put the thought into words. "He went to see Old ABC!" she exclaimed.

Sheriff Brandon's excitement brought him to his feet. "Now," he said, "we're *really* getting somewhere. We're figuring out exactly what happened. Old ABC has been the leading criminal lawyer on the Pacific Coast for a long time. Carleton Grines came out here. He went to jail in Oregon. He associated with crooks. They told him, 'If you ever get in a jam, go to Old ABC. He can get you out – if you've got the money.' Well, you can see what happened. Grines forgot who he was for ten years. Then he came out of his trance and realized that something had happened. He found thirty-five thousand dollars in his pocket. It never occurred to him that he could have become so affluent he could go to a bank and draw out thirty-five thousand dollars in cash, and that the money was really his own. The only explanation he could think of was that he'd been mixed up in some crime and that his share of the 'take' was thirty-five thousand dollars.

"He knew he was wanted by the police for that jail break. He felt certain he'd been mixed up in some big crime – so he went to ABC to find out what it was all about and get Carr to tell him what to do. He didn't have much difficulty in locating Carr, looked up his name in a telephone book, found his office address, inquired there for his residence address, and was advised that he was living in Madison City."

"Then, when he went to Carr's," Sylvia Martin said thoughtfully, "he was murdered, and the thirty-five thousand disappeared."

"It isn't as simple as that," Selby pointed out. "He went to Las Alidas."

"Before or after he went to see Carr?" Brandon asked.

Selby said, "We don't know."

"Yes, we do, Doug," Sylvia rushed on eagerly. "It *must* have been after he saw Carr the first time … Carr must have put through a long-distance telephone call to the brother in Oklahoma, found out he was visiting in Las Alidas, and told his client to go over there, but Carleton got to drinking … No, wait a minute. He must have gone to Las Alidas to see the brother. No one answered the bell, and he picked up the car that was sitting in the driveway. It had an Oklahoma licence, so he thought it was his brother's automobile. He started uptown, got to drinking, headed back toward Carr's place, became drunk, and – "

Selby said, "You keep making it too simple. When he was in Las Alidas he knew he was Billmeyer. He telephoned Carmen Freelman, asked her to meet him, and when she came to Las Alidas, asked her to give him an alibi.

"Now Billmeyer wouldn't have done that. That was Carleton Grines, the crook, asking for an alibi. And that means he was planning some crime for which he wanted an alibi.

"But at that time he was also being Billmeyer. So we get back to the fact that when he recovered his memory, he also remembered the Billmeyer part – and that doesn't agree with the evidence of the tweed suit, the missing thirty-five thousand dollars or the trip to see ABC – if he did go there.

"So the evidence is all cockeyed, or else we – "

The ringing of the telephone interrupted him.

Sheriff Brandon picked up the instrument. "Hello. Yes, Perkins … Well, just a minute, Harry. Doug's here now. Let me ask him."

Brandon turned to Doug Selby. "Harry Perkins on the line," he said. "A Los Angeles reporter by the name of Joe Raft, and a man with him who seems to be a scientist of some sort, wants to examine the tweed suit of clothes that Billmeyer was wearing when his body was picked up. Perkins wants to know if it's all right."

Selby grinned triumphantly. "Tell Perkins that it's all right provided we're there. Raft can see that suit of clothes *in our presence*."

Brandon nodded, said into the telephone, "We're comin' right down, Harry. Stall him off until we get there. We want to be present when he looks that suit over."

Brandon hung up the telephone and grinned at Selby. "Okay, son," he said. "It's bein' dumped right in our laps. Raft thinks he's got the case solved. The solution depends on that suit of clothes. He's tipped his hand now."

Sylvia Martin was halfway to the door. "Well, Mister District Attorney, you've called the turn. It *was* that suit of clothes. It's that bit of evidence that holds a key to the solution. Come on. Let's go and find out what they want."

Joseph Bagley Raft was a medium-sized man in the late thirties. His eyes were dark, quick in their motions, and gave the impression of taking everything in, just as his thin, tight-lipped mouth gave the impression of letting nothing out. As Brandon said afterward, "He acts like a guy in a tight game of draw poker who has just filled a straight flush."

Harry Perkins performed the introductions.

Raft at first paid but little attention to Selby and Brandon. Quite evidently he regarded them from the viewpoint of a high-priced city reporter meeting two unsophisticated country officials who were, for the moment, offering a temporary obstruction to his investigations.

For Sylvia Martin, Raft had that second glance which men give to a pretty woman; and then Perkins added to the formal introduction, "You'd oughta know Miss Martin. She's a reporter, too."

For a moment Raft stiffened. His lips smiled, but the expression remained carved on his face. "Local paper?" he asked.

"*The Clarion*," Sylvia said.

"Oh, yes."

Perkins introduced Raft's companion, a Mr Bemexter.

Sylvia Martin flashed Doug a significant glance. "Are you a reporter, too, Mr Bemexter?" she asked.

Bemexter's smile was cordial, but he was delightfully vague in his reply. "I'm afraid I haven't the necessary ability to be a reporter."

"Or a lawyer?" Brandon asked.

"No."

Selby said, smiling dryly, "Perhaps you're related to the Thomas L Bemexter who wrote the book on criminology. What was the title of it? Oh, yes, *Solving Murders With the Microscope*."

Bemexter's smile was equally dry. "I am afraid I'll have to plead guilty," he said.

Raft looked Selby over with the air of a man making a second and more complete appraisal. Quite evidently he hadn't intended to let anyone know that he was bringing a high-priced consulting criminologist into the case.

"They want to look at Billmeyer's clothes," Perkins explained.

"May I ask why?" Selby asked.

Raft did the talking for the visitors. Quite evidently he expected to do it all. "We're interested in solving the puzzle – the crime, if there was a crime."

"That's fine," Selby said. "I'll certainly welcome the assistance of a man of such ability and reputation as Mr Bemexter … I take it he'll tell us anything he may find out?"

"Oh, certainly," Raft said.

"Give us a copy of his report?"

"He'll be glad to."

Selby smiled. "When?"

"Well," Raft said, his eyes twinkling, "we'd mail you a copy of the report just as soon as we had it."

"Which would put it in my office about the time your paper hit the streets?" Selby asked.

"Just about," Raft admitted.

"And we wouldn't get it until then."

Raft said, "Let's be frank, Mr Selby. Bemexter's services cost money. There's an angle of this I want to investigate. I want Bemexter's opinion. My paper's paying for that. Naturally, my paper isn't making a charitable contribution to Madison County so that our competitors will get the information at the same time we do – and perhaps publish it first."

"Suppose," Selby asked, "this is a murder case, and suppose the murderer should escape because we didn't have the information in time to act on it?"

Raft said, "I'll tell you what I'll do, Mr Selby. I'll guarantee that one hour before our newspaper hits the streets you'll have all the information ... You can't very well ask us to do more than that. Remember that if it weren't for us, you wouldn't get this information at all."

"Let him see the suit," Selby said to Harry Perkins.

Perkins, who had been holding Fido on his lap, dropped him to the floor, said, "Okay, here we are."

He unlocked a metal locker, brought out the clothes Billmeyer had been wearing when the body was recovered from the automobile.

Bemexter stepped forward, instantly began working. He opened a suitcase which seemed to be crammed with various and sundry electric paraphernalia. He said to the coroner, "I'd like to unscrew one of these lights and plug some apparatus in the socket."

"Go right ahead," Perkins said.

The little group gathered around the bench on which Bemexter placed the clothes, watched him unscrew a light globe, insert a double socket. In one of the sockets he placed a shaded light which gave a brilliant, slightly bluish illumination. In the other he plugged a cord, took a small vacuum cleaner from the suitcase, hooked up the vacuum cleaner, tore open a sealed envelope, took out a clean, white sack, inserted this into a compartment of the cleaner, and started the motor. With deft skill he ran this cleaner around the cuff of the left trousers leg.

When he had finished he carefully removed the sack with whatever had been recovered from the left cuff, sealed it, wrote on it, "Left trousers cuff, X-21," and dropped it into his suitcase.

While he was opening another envelope and putting another sack on the vacuum cleaner, Brandon. asked, "What's the X-21 mean?"

"It's a key number that I've given this case," Bemexter explained crisply. "That saves putting the date, locality, persons present, and everything on each envelope. I enter all that in a notebook under the key number X-21."

"I see."

Bemexter deftly extracted whatever dust there was from the right trousers cuff and put that in an envelope. He next ran the vacuum cleaner under the collar of the coat; then he studied the cuffs of the trousers and the ends of the sleeves under a microscope.

A stain on one of the sleeves demanded his thoughtful attention. He pulled a switch on the light, and instantly the sleeve was bathed in an ultraviolet illumination under which the criminologist examined the stain from different angles; then he switched the regular light back on and ran the vacuum cleaner over the entire suit.

Raft tried to divert the attention of his audience. "Well," he said, "that's about all there is to it, just a glorified job of cleaning … What do you do with that stuff, Bemexter?"

"Examine it under a microscope," Bemexter said curtly.

"Well," Raft said, "I guess there's nothing to be gained by sticking around watching you," and ostentatiously crossed over to the other end of the room to sit on the corner of a table. He lit a cigarette and called across to Sylvia Martin, "*The Clarion's* a morning paper, isn't it?"

"Yes," she said, without taking her eyes from what Bemexter was doing.

When Bemexter finished with the tweed suit he examined the shoes carefully, taking scrapings from the inside of the heel, from around the edges of the stitching on the soles. He examined the shoe laces with the greatest care.

Raft sat over on the corner of the table and smoked, trying to inveigle the others into conversation; but while they replied to his questions, they kept a close watch on Bemexter.

The criminologist examined the socks, called for the underwear, and then, at the very last, turned the pockets of the tweed suit inside out and collected whatever bits of dust he could find in the corners of those pockets with his vacuum cleaner.

"Got everything you want?" Raft asked as Bemexter pulled the cord out of the socket.

"I think so."

"Okay," Raft announced. "How long will it take you to make your examination?"

"It depends on what I find," Bemexter said vaguely.

Raft said, "Well, I guess that's it. Thanks a lot, Mr Selby. Ever so much obliged to you for co-operating."

Bemexter unscrewed his double socket, returned the light globe to the place from which it had been taken, stored his things in his suitcase, said to Selby, "Let me leave you one of my cards. It might come in handy sometime."

"Thanks," Selby said, taking the card.

"You have one of my books?"

"Yes."

"Glad you remembered it."

Raft took Bemexter's arm, all but hurried him through the door. "Well, thanks a lot, fellows."

When they had gone Perkins said, "By gosh, I'm wonderin'. They've breezed in here and taken whatever evidence there was in that suit away with them."

Selby said, "It's nothing we could have worked on with our limited equipment. It takes microscopes, cameras – in short, a whole crime laboratory."

"If you *hadn't* let him see the suit," Sylvia said to Perkins, "Raft would have turned on the heat. His paper would have made it seem that Doug and Rex Brandon were virtually shielding the murderer. *The Blade* would have taken up the hue and cry, and made the whole county administration seem ridiculous."

Perkins nodded.

Selby said, "I notice that he seemed to have finished with the suit before he went back to examine the pockets."

"And during that time Raft tried to decoy us over to the other end of the room," Sylvia pointed out.

Selby pulled his pipe from his pocket, slid the fastener back on his tobacco pouch, and crammed fragrant tobacco into the dark bowl.

"I'm wondering," he said, "if Raft was really trying to decoy us away. He seemed just a little obvious about it."

"Of course, he was," Brandon said. "He went over and sat on the table and said there wasn't going to be anything to look at – tried to get us to come over there and talk to him."

"I don't know," Selby said. "Raft is clever. I'm wondering if he may not have deliberately made it seem he was *trying* to divert our attention, so that we'd refuse to have it diverted, and look at the suit of clothes all the more intently."

"I don't get you, son," the sheriff said.

"Something else he wanted," Selby pointed out; "wanted to get something without our knowing it. He – "

"He couldn't," Perkins interrupted. "I keep everything locked up here. That's one thing that I'm always careful about. Can't ever tell when somebody's going to try to slip something out, so I keep things under lock and key ... He never went near my desk, sat on the corner of the table over there."

Selby said, "The more I think of it, the more I feel certain he was deliberately trying to fool us – get us into the frame of mind where we were determined to see every single move Bemexter made ... What was over here?"

"I tell you, there wasn't anything."

Abruptly Selby muttered an exclamation.

"What?" Perkins asked.

"I'll bet I have it! The one clue we've all been overlooking."

"What?"

"The dog."

Perkins stared at him as though he thought the district attorney had gone crazy.

"Don't you see?" Selby exclaimed. "I've been blind – asleep at the switch. The most important clue in the whole case. The dog!"

"What's the dog got to do with it? How could *he* be the most important clue?" Perkins asked.

"The dog didn't belong to the people in that car," Selby said excitedly. "The dog probably has a habit of jumping in cars. Even so, it would hardly have rushed out from the sidewalk and jumped into a strange car, but if the dog had been thrown from an automobile and was rather dazed, he would have climbed into – Of course! The dog *was in the car with the corpse.*"

"Then the dog belonged to Billmeyer," Sylvia Martin exclaimed.

"That doesn't necessarily follow," Selby pointed out.

"Raft was petting the dog over here," Brandon admitted.

Selby dropped down to his knees, called, "Come on, Fido. Come over here."

The dog came over to him, wagging his tail. Selby started scratching behind his ears with his fingertips, at the same time running his hand quickly over the dog's coat.

"Here it is," he said abruptly.

"What?" Perkins asked.

Selby held the dog around so that they could see.

A small furrow of the dog's hair had been cut away, apparently with very sharp pocket scissors.

Brandon said, "Hold on a minute, Doug. You're going too fast for me."

Selby, talking rapidly in his excitement, said, "Raft cut that hair from the dog and slipped it in an envelope in his pocket."

"Why?"

"Because that suit is tied up with the dog – and the dog and the suit are connected with the murderer."

"You mean with the murderer or with the victim?"

"With the murderer."

"How come?"

"When Carleton Grines escaped from jail, he'd been convicted of a crime and was serving a sentence … Now, what happens to a man's clothes when he goes to jail?"

"They take 'em off," Brandon said, "and give him overalls. Usually, it's overalls made by sewing different coloured cloth together. The ones *we* use are half brown and half blue."

"Exactly. I didn't make inquiries from the Oregon authorities about that, but they must have some distinctive type of clothes they give prisoners to wear while they're in the jail. The jail burned up. There was no chance for Grines to get his own clothes. They must have burned up in the jail."

"But this suit didn't burn up."

"That's it. Grines must have had a new suit. He must have worn it when he was convicted. This suit was in someone's possession. Whose?"

"The wife's!" Sylvia exclaimed.

"That's the logical deduction, all right."

"Oh oh!" Brandon said. "Now, the puzzle begins to fit together."

Selby went on, "Acting on the theory that Carleton Grines had put this suit away somewhere and then lost the Grines identity and become Billmeyer, he couldn't have had access to this suit. If he had, the first thing he'd have looked for would have been letters in the pockets. Here was a letter with his brother's return address on it ... It begins to look very much as though the dog and the suit were tied up with Mrs Carleton Grines."

"And that's what Raft was after?" Sylvia asked.

"Probably Raft was looking for dog hairs on the suit. Once he finds them, then it means the dog is connected with the murderer. He probably knows all about the dog already."

Brandon said, "It looks like we go to call on Mrs Carleton Grines."

"Got a leash for that dog, Harry?" Selby asked the coroner.

"You won't need any leash," Perkins said. "All you have to do is open the door of an automobile and he'll jump in ... That's evidently what happened down there at the intersection the night of the smash-up."

Selby said, "I'll want to take him into a house with me. Guess I'll just carry him under my arm."

He picked up the coroner's telephone and dialled the number of Inez Stapleton's apartment.

He heard the ringing of the telephone bell; then as Inez picked up the receiver, heard the tail end of a sentence she was finishing. "... a most important witness," she said, and then into the telephone, "Hello?"

"Hello, Inez. This is Doug."

"Oh, hello, Doug."

"I wonder if it's too late for me to run up. I want to talk with you."

"Doug! I'd love it!" Then suddenly the animation went out of her voice. "Business, I suppose?" she asked.

"In a way, yes. The sheriff's with me, and – "

Doug looked up to catch Sylvia Martin's gesture which indicated she was checking out.

"There are a couple of questions I'd like to ask you," he said into the telephone.

Inez Stapleton's voice was as crisp as a cold lettuce leaf. "I'm engaged right at present, Doug, but if you could make it in about an hour and a half, I think it would be all right."

"All right, we'll be there," Selby said, and hung up the telephone.

Sylvia said, "I'll check out of the party when you go up there, Doug. I couldn't do any good, and my being along might do some harm."

"All right. I'll bet she's talking with her client right now. Someone was up there."

Brandon said, "We'll try and get the dog into the apartment, and then watch the way he acts. If he belongs to Mrs Carleton Grines, he can still get her scent there in the apartment. He'll start barking and whining."

Selby nodded thoughtfully, "Don't let her know we're making a test with the dog, Rex. We'll pretend we're just taking him along. We can ..."

"What is it?" the sheriff asked as Doug became suddenly silent.

"I'm wondering if we're not getting the cart before the horse."

"How come?"

"We're thinking about Billmeyer's wife, Mrs Carleton Grines. Let's do a little thinking about some of the other people – the brother, for instance."

"What about him?"

127

Selby said, "Everything about the suit and the dog could tie in with the brother. We'd just about have time to run over to Las Alidas and drop in on Hinkle and Mr and Mrs Pervis Grines. We could take the dog with us and see what happens."

Brandon said, "Somehow, Doug, I like that idea better than the other one. There's something about Hinkle and Pervis Grines ... And it was Hinkle's car Billmeyer was driving. Don't forget that."

Selby nodded thoughtfully, said to the dog, "Come on, Fido. You're going home. You understand? Home."

The dog perked up his ears, twisted his head, first to the left, then to the right.

"Home," Selby repeated.

The dog barked.

Sylvia was all but dancing with excitement. "Oh, come on, Doug! Let's go! That dog is the ace card Raft is holding up his sleeve, and if you can only beat him to it – if you *only* can."

Perkins held the door open for them.

The rain was beating down in torrents, dripping from the roof of the porch, whipping along the sidewalk in sheets, sending up little geysers of water from the pavement.

Selby scooped the dog under his overcoat. "Come on, Fido. You're going for a ride."

The little group scuttled down the rain-drenched walk to scramble pell-mell into the big county car.

Wind was coming up steadily, whipping the rain in sheets.

The main street of Las Alidas seemed bleak and deserted. The persons who were doing their Saturday night shopping or coming into town for the movies hurried quickly across the rain-pelted sidewalks.

The neon signs threw a reddish glow up into the misty darkness. The steady thrumming of raindrops furnished a monotonous undertone of sound upon which was imposed the higher pitched noises of tyres hissing along the pavement.

"Want to pick up Billy Ransome?" Sheriff Brandon asked, turning toward the back seat where Doug was sitting, holding the dog.

"Not now. Let's just go around by Hinkle's and see what the dog does. It may be a false alarm."

"Don't you ever think it's a false alarm," Sylvia Martin said. "I say it's like betting on a sure thing. It was Hinkle's car and – "

Selby said, "We'll drive around and see if the dog shows any sign of recognizing the neighbourhood. I'll hold him up so he can see out."

Brandon turned to the left on Chestnut Street, drove several blocks, said, "How's the pooch doin', Doug?"

Selby said, "Slow down a bit, Rex. I'm not certain he can see out of the window."

"Roll the window down," Sylvia said. "Let him get the *smell* of the neighbourhood. He can tell more by that."

Selby rolled down the window on the lee side.

Rain, pelting on the car door, sent fine spray through the window. The dog pushed out his head, started sniffing.

"It's going to work," Sylvia Martin exclaimed. "He knows the neighbourhood. He knows where he is all right!"

They reached the six hundred block on Chestnut Street.

Selby said, "He doesn't seem very enthusiastic."

"It's on account of the rain," Brandon said. "I'll drive around the block and come up on the house from the other way."

He turned the car. Sylvia asked, "Did you notice the car that was parked in Hinkle's driveway?"

"I didn't," Selby admitted. "I was watching the dog."

"I just saw a car was there," Brandon said over his shoulder. "What about it, Sylvia?"

"Unless I'm greatly mistaken, that auto belongs to A B Carr," she said.

Brandon turned the corner. "If Old ABC is visiting at that house," he announced, "*we're* going to drop in on the party."

"Keep your temper, Rex," Selby warned. "Carr's shrewd, and you don't get anywhere with him by getting mad."

"I know," Brandon growled, "but some day I'm going to disconnect his head from his backbone. How's the pooch doing, Doug?"

Selby laughed bitterly. "He's settled down and gone to sleep. Another good hunch gone wrong."

Brandon said, "Okay, we'll turn down this next street and go back Chestnut."

The next street, however, was closed. Not until they reached the fourth cross street did they find one which was open.

Sylvia gave a little exclamation of disappointment. "The car isn't there now, Rex."

Brandon gently put on the brakes, eased the car to a stop. "You're sure it was Carr's automobile, Sylvia?"

"Pretty sure."

"There's a light in the house," Selby pointed out. "Let's go on in and see what Hinkle has to say for himself. We won't say anything about Carr's having been here – not for a few minutes. We'll see if Hinkle volunteers the information."

"How's the pooch coming along?" Brandon asked.

"Still asleep," Selby said. "We'll roll the windows down just far enough to give him some air ... Okay, let's go."

They got out into the beating rain.

Sylvia gathered up her skirts under the raincoat, and sprinted for the porch. Selby and the sheriff came sloshing along more slowly. Sylvia was ringing the doorbell by the time they reached the steps leading up to the porch.

Hinkle opened the door. "What do you want? Oh, I get you now ... The DA and the sheriff. Come in."

"Miss Martin," Selby introduced.

"Well, come on in," Hinkle said. "It seems to be my night for visitors."

"What's the matter?" Selby asked, glancing at Brandon.

"Well," Hinkle said, "one just left. He – " Abruptly he stopped. Selby waited for him to go on, but Hinkle said instead, "Come on in here. Pervis and Ruth are in here."

Pervis Grines got up, said, "Hello. Anything the matter? I suppose you saw *The Blade* tonight. I think that whole thing is a frame-up. Carleton never married that woman."

Hinkle said, "Won't you folks sit down?"

Mrs Grines said with some feeling, "We're going to fight that scheming woman every inch of the way. We've got the best lawyer in the state, A B Carr."

Selby said, "Isn't Carr representing Mrs Gilbert Freelman?"

"She hasn't any interest in it," Mrs Grines said.

"And she's not on trial for anything," her husband interpolated.

"It's the brother he's representing. He – "

Hinkle coughed significantly.

"So he's going to represent you in the fight over the estate," Selby commented, apparently not noticing the unfinished sentence.

"Yes."

"The lawyer on the other side," Selby pointed out, "is rather clever. Inez Stapleton. She's hard working and sincere."

"Poof!" Mrs Grines said. "We're not afraid of her. Why, Mr Carr dropped in to see her tonight just before he came over here, and she – "

Once more Hinkle coughed.

Pervis Grines said suddenly, "Perhaps we'd better let Carr do the talking for us, Ruth."

"Why, of course," Mrs Grines said, "but, good heavens, there's no harm in telling them that he's representing us. They'll read about that in the paper."

"By the way," Selby observed casually, "what do you think of Carmen Freelman's brother?"

"Oh, he's all right, but his trouble doesn't have anything to do with our case. There's no reason why Mr Carr can't represent us and still represent him."

"You don't think there's any conflict in your interests?" Selby asked, apparently surprised.

"Absolutely not. Even if there was, in order to get Carr we'd be willing to concede – "

Hinkle's fit of coughing was violent and prolonged.

Mrs Grines waited for him to finish, said, "I told them that – "

Pervis Grines interrupted, "I think you're talking too damn much, Ruth."

"Oh, you do!" she exclaimed. "Well, I guess I know what I can say and what I can't say. I'm not telling them anything about the really big thing. I have as much right – "

"Take it easy, Ruth," Pervis cautioned. "We're playing for big stakes now. We don't want to boot our chances … I tell you what, Mr Selby. You go talk with A B Carr. He'll tell you everything that you want to know – everything that wouldn't interfere with our side of the case."

"Personally," Mrs Grines said, "I don't think there is any other side."

"Don't kid yourself," Hinkle observed.

"You're up against a woman who claims to be the widow, and you're up against a woman who is acting as her lawyer. That woman, from all I can hear, is pretty well thought of in this county. You get up in front of a jury with some women on it, and let that lady lawyer start doing a little tear jerking about how the poor wife was scrimping and sacrificing during ten long years while her husband was amassing a fortune and gratifying his every wish – "

"Scrimping, my eye!" Ruth interrupted. "I'll bet if we put detectives on her trail the way Carr suggests and – "

Pervis Grines said ominously, "Now listen, Ruth, you're all steamed up about this thing and *you're talking too much*. This is *my* business, and you're *my* wife. I guess I have something to say about what's going to be done."

"You remember the last thing Carr said when he left," Hinkle reminded them. "He said not to talk to anyone."

Ruth Grines became sullen.

"Oh, all right," she said, "if you put it that way, I won't say a word. But I think you're making a mistake. There's no reason at all why we shouldn't help the officers. We may want information from them before we get done."

She sat angrily silent, cheeks flushed, eyes staring straight down at the carpet.

Pervis Grines said to Selby, "I'm sorry, but that's the way it is. You're a lawyer yourself. You know how *you'd* feel if you had a half-million-dollar lawsuit and your clients got to talking too much."

Selby said, "I wouldn't like it."

"That's just the way I feel about it – and I don't think Carr's going to like it. And that woman reporter's taking notes of everything we've said."

Mrs Grines said angrily, "As though I'd told him something! Good heavens, you'd think I'd – "

"Nix on it," Pervis Grines warned.

There was a moment of awkward silence, then Grines said in a more conciliatory tone, "If there's anything you want to find out about, you can reach Carr at his home."

"Not now, you can't," Ruth said. "If you're going to do the talking, why don't you tell it straight?"

"He said he was going home," Grines said, "that we could reach him there if – "

"But not for an hour. He was going through El – "

Hinkle interrupted to say, "I don't want to butt into this thing, but just suppose these men happen to be interested in – "

He paused. His eyes, looking around the room, finally came to rest on a table on which were a bottle of ink, a steel pen, and a blotter. He finished his sentence by nodding at that table.

Selby said, "Don't misunderstand me, please. I have absolutely no interest in the outcome of litigation affecting the Billmeyer estate. I don't care anything about the facts except so far as they relate to the cause of Billmeyer's death. So far as that is concerned, I am the district attorney of this county, and the sheriff and I are going to get every bit of evidence we can uncover. Is that plain?"

"That's plain," Hinkle said.

"And fair," Grines added, "and, under the circumstances, we aren't saying anything more."

Selby got up from his chair, said, "And that leaves me with just one thing to say. It's good night."

Grines grinned. "Well, we'll meet you halfway on that," he said, "and say good night ourselves."

Grines held the door open for them.

They ran out through the pelting rain to the damp interior of the county car.

Fido, curled up on the seat asleep, looked up, gave his tail a couple of thumps, stretched himself erect, yawned, looked out of the window, and touched the back of Selby's wet hand with his tongue.

The door slammed shut. The porch light clicked off, and, for a moment, the only sound was the pelting of rain on the roof of the county car.

"Well," Brandon said, stepping on the starter, "I guess that's that."

Selby, in a low voice, said, "Swing around in a U-turn, and step on it, Rex."

"Going to see ABC?" Brandon asked.

Selby said, "We're going to make all the time we can to El Bocano."

"What's the idea?" the sheriff asked.

Selby said, "Old ABC wants in on that estate fight. There's a chance for him to pick up a huge fee. He's representing Milton Gregory, Carmen's brother, in connection with something that has to do with the estate.

"He took Gregory over there and presented an agreement for all of them to sign, an agreement that there wouldn't be any conflict in interests, and that Carr could represent both parties. That's why the bottle of ink and the pen were on the table, and Milton Gregory is the person Hinkle had in mind when he paused in the middle of a sentence and finished it by jerking his head over toward the ink bottle on the table.

"And because Mrs Grines carefully avoided mentioning that Gregory had been there with Carr, she thought she was keeping the secret."

Brandon gave a low whistle.

"What's more," Selby went on, "Carr wasn't going directly back to Madison City. He was going to drive to El Bocano. Mrs Grines let that slip. They stopped her before she mentioned the name of the city, but she did let the first syllable slip out."

Sylvia Martin squeezed Doug's shoulder.

Brandon said, "*That* would explain it. That's what Hinkle was so afraid she was going to spill, and she thought she was keeping it covered up ... What do you suppose Milton Gregory has to do with it, Doug?"

"That," Selby said, "is going to be very, very interesting – and one other thing is going to be interesting."

"What's the other thing, Doug?"

"Whether Old ABC deposits any one-thousand-dollar bills in his bank on Monday morning."

Chapter Fourteen

The first torrential downpour of the storm had settled into a cold, dispiriting drizzle which made the reflections of El Bocano's street lights shimmer in cold ribbons from the wet pavements.

Here in the agricultural community, despite the wartime restrictions, Saturday night remained the big night, a night when people came to town to buy and sell supplies, see the movies, and form in little groups, discussing current affairs.

The sheriff slowed for the traffic.

"Any ideas?" Brandon asked Selby.

"No," Selby said, "unless we happen to run onto his car parked somewhere on the main street – or unless we get a lead at the hotel."

They drove up and down the length of the main Street, crawling along, noticing the parked automobiles.

"Looks as though we'll have to try the hotel," Selby said. "It certainly is damp and chilly ... Park right in front of the hotel there, Rex. I'll run in and see if I can get a lead."

"Would it be better if I did it," Sylvia asked. "I could make a casual inquiry; if either you or the sheriff – "

"Good idea," Selby told her. "Skip on in and check up on the register. Notice the last two or three names. Ask a few questions about the last man who registered."

Brandon stopped the car, left the motor running, the windshield wipers clicking back and forth.

"Heater's broken on the bus," Brandon explained as Sylvia Martin crossed the sidewalk to enter the lighted lobby of the hotel. "Haven't been able to get any parts to repair it. Certainly is cold in the car."

Selby fished his tobacco pouch from his pocket, pushed tobacco into the blackened bowl of his brier. "Well," he said, "we're getting on the right track, anyway. Carr knows something, and Carr is greedy. Of course, he's too slick to let us catch him soliciting business in an unethical manner, but if we only knew the truth of – "

He broke off as Sylvia Martin came to the doorway of the hotel, beckoning eagerly.

"Looks like we've struck pay dirt," Brandon said, switching off the headlights and the motor.

They crossed the wet sidewalk. Sylvia Martin, standing in the doorway, said in a low voice, "He's in room 406. I'm certain it's the man we want."

"Carr there?" Selby asked.

"No. A tall man came into the hotel with him while he registered, then left. That must have been Carr. Gregory is registered under the name of Frank Carmody."

Selby grinned. "We go right up," he said, "without being announced."

A dispirited automatic elevator rattled and shivered its way to the fourth and top floor. They found the room they wanted without difficulty, and Selby knocked.

They could see light coming through the top of the transom, but there was no answer until Selby knocked the second time; then a man's voice said, "Who is it?"

"Message," Selby said.

"Put it under the door."

Selby said, "Open the door, Gregory. This message is from the law."

The silence from the other side of the door was so prolonged that Brandon, inching his way forward, said, "Open that door, or we'll break it down."

A bolt shot back, and Milton Gregory, his face twitching with nervousness, said, "What do you want?"

"We want to talk with you," Selby said.

Rex Brandon, shouldering past him, pushed his way into the room.

"You can't do this," Gregory said. "You haven't any right. You can't come in here. You – "

Brandon put a heavy hand on the young man's shoulder. "We've already done it," he said. "Sit down."

Under the pressure of Brandon's strong arm, Milton Gregory sat down abruptly in a straight-backed chair.

Brandon stood over him. "Would you rather be arrested for murder," he asked, "or tell us the truth?"

"*Murder!*"

"That's what I said."

"You haven't got anything on me."

Brandon's laugh was scornful.

"I just tried to protect my sister," Gregory said.

Selby, stepping forward, said, "That isn't what Pervis Grines tells us."

He saw dismay on the young man's face and followed up his lead. "We just came from there," he said, and then added casually, "Have you got a copy of that agreement you signed, or did Carr take it?"

"Carr took it."

Selby slipped off his raincoat, dropped it over the foot of the bed, and sat down. "All right, Gregory," he said casually, "start talking."

"You can't do this to me."

Brandon said, "I'm getting tired of hearing that."

"What do you want, anyway?"

"We want the truth," Selby said.

"I'm not making any statement."

"Listen," Selby said, getting to his feet and pointing his finger at Milton Gregory, "Billmeyer didn't call your sister until after you had called her. It was *your* call that frightened her. I'm going to put the cards right out on the table. You're absolutely correct when you say that we haven't anything on you – yet. But we can get something on you, and when we do I don't propose to have you in a sanitarium with a nervous breakdown. We've got enough on you to hold you for investigation, and you either talk now or you get in the county car, go to jail, and let your lawyer get you out on a writ of *habeas corpus*, in which event we'll have enough bail put up to make certain that you're around when we want you."

"You can't put a charge against me – not in *this* county."

Brandon said, "You're a material witness and – "

Selby interrupted, "We co-operate pretty closely with the authorities in Los Angeles. We don't care what jail you're in just so we know where we can put our finger on you."

All of the fight oozed out of Gregory. Brandon saw what was happening, took off his raincoat, sat down, and said, "That's better."

Sylvia Martin gravitated toward a dark corner of the room, drew out a chair, and made herself inconspicuous.

"Go ahead," Selby said. "Start talking."

"I'm not guilty of any crime," Gregory said. "I didn't intend to deceive anybody. I never thought there would be any trouble – definitely. I thought that cheque was good as gold."

"I know," Selby said, "you made a mistake; but you can't expect us to be very sympathetic the way you've played things."

"It seemed like the only thing to do at the time."

"Well, circumstances are different now. Suppose you give us all the details."

Gregory, speaking with nervous rapidity, said, "I had this cheque for fifteen hundred dollars. I needed the money bad. The cheque was on an eastern bank, and I couldn't get the cash on it. They wanted to put it through for collection. That would have meant a delay. I simply had to have that money. I'd been counting on it. The cheque had been delayed and – "

"What did you do?" Selby asked.

"I wanted Sis to endorse it, but I couldn't get hold of her, and – "

"So you forged her signature?" Brandon asked as he faltered.

It was Selby who interpreted correctly the young man's silence. "He forged Billmeyer's signature," he charged.

"It wasn't a forgery," Gregory insisted. "I never intended to stick him for it. All I wanted was to get that cheque through the bank. I just wrote 'okay' on it and Billmeyer's signature under that. Honestly, I never had any idea that cheque would be dishonoured. The man who gave it to me was good as gold and – "

"And when the cheque was dishonoured, you rang up your sister and told her about it?"

"I told her that we had to get in touch with Billmeyer, that I had to explain it to him, that something had to be done. The cheque came in Wednesday afternoon. The bank got in touch with me. They told me that I had until Friday noon to make it good; then they'd collect from Mr Billmeyer on his endorsement … I tried to get the money somewhere else before I called Sis."

"And," Selby said, "Billmeyer, not knowing anything about the cheque, would have had you in jail an hour after they'd made the demand."

"No, he wouldn't," Gregory said sullenly. "He'd have used it to bring pressure to bear on Sis."

"Oh, so *that* was it."

Gregory nodded.

Selby glanced at Brandon, then turned back to Gregory. "That all of it?"

"Isn't that enough?"

"It's too much, if you ask me, but I'm asking you for facts."

"That's all of it," Gregory said.

"What happened?"

"Sis told me she didn't think there was anything she could do. She said that Billmeyer had been – well, he'd been making a play for her, wanted her to go away with him. It was a mess."

"So you went to A B Carr?"

"Yes."

"How did you happen to go to him?"

"I'd heard of him. I'd known a few people who went to him when they were in a jam. He got them out. It costs money, but he can deliver the goods."

"All right, you went to Carr. Then what?"

"You know the rest."

"Did your sister know you'd gone to Carr?"

"Yes."

Selby thought things over for a few moments. "I see," he said. "So when Carmen saw Billmeyer's body, she thought that you had done it."

Gregory squirmed uncomfortably in the chair, but didn't say anything.

"So she went to Carr to find out just what *had* happened, and Carr, realizing that that forgery made an excellent motive for murder and wanting to keep the whole thing hushed up, suggested that she get out of circulation and that everybody swear the endorsement on the cheque was genuine. Then the fifteen hundred dollars would be collected from the estate, and everybody would be satisfied."

Gregory remained doggedly silent.

"That it?" Selby asked.

"Well, something like that – only he didn't tell that to Sis."

"Who did he tell it to?"

"Me."

"What did you do?"

"I persuaded Sis she should put herself in charge of this doctor and go to a sanitarium until she could get her nerves under control."

"How did you happen to kill Billmeyer?" Selby asked. "How did you get him to take that drink – "

"I didn't kill him."

Selby went on remorselessly, "You got in touch with your sister. Your sister told him about that cheque and suggested that he should get together with you. He was to meet you somewhere up there in Orange Heights, perhaps at Carr's residence. You drugged him and intended to smash up his automobile so it would look as though he died in an automobile wreck, but he had a weak heart, and the drugged drink – "

"You're crazy! I never did any such thing. I never even saw him," Gregory said.

"Got an alibi?" Selby inquired.

"You can talk to Carr about that."

"We're talking to you now."

"I'm not going to say anything more."

"Don't you think you'd better make an explanation – not only for your own sake, but for your sister's sake?"

Gregory shook his head. "I've said everything I'm going to. I've explained everything."

"And so you went out to see Pervis Grines. You may or may not have told the whole truth to Grines, but in any event Carr had an agreement all worked out by which Grines agreed that he wouldn't prosecute you, that the estate would pay that cheque, and that because no charge would be made there wouldn't be any reason why Carr couldn't represent Pervis Grines in trying to keep Billmeyer's widow from getting the estate. Is that right?"

"If you know so much about it," Gregory said with a sudden burst of anger, "why are you asking me?"

"I want to get your story."

"You've got it."

"I want all of it."

"You've got it all – all you're going to get."

Selby nodded to Brandon. "Under the circumstances, Rex, I guess the only thing to do is to arrest him."

"You can't arrest me for forgery. Grines says it's okay. He won't – "

"We can arrest you for suspicion of murder," Selby said.

Gregory came up out of the chair, fighting with the desperation of sheer panic. "You're going to try and frame it on me! You and your damn political stooge! You think you can hang this murder around my neck, and – " His fists lashed out.

Brandon side-stepped neatly, caught the young man's wrist in a grip of steel, bent his arm back. The ratchets of the handcuffs clicked. Brandon stepped away and left Milton Gregory, white-faced and shaken, struggling against the grip of the steel bracelets.

Moving with calm unconcern, Brandon walked over to the closet, opened the door, took out the young man's hat and coat, put the hat on his head, threw the coat over his shoulders. "Now then," he said, "if you keep your mouth shut and don't try to act smart, no one will know there's anything wrong when we walk through the lobby. When we get in the car, I'll handcuff your wrists in front of you ... All right, young man, let's go."

When they had their prisoner lodged in the county jail, Brandon looked at his watch and said to Selby, "You're late for that appointment, Doug."

"I know, but I can't help it. We'll get away from here right away."

Milton Gregory said, "All right, you wise guys, you've thrown me in without any charge being placed against me. I demand that I have an opportunity to communicate with my attorney, A B Carr."

"You're within your rights in making *that* demand," Brandon told him with a smile. "The jailer will put through a call for you."

The jailer looked at the sheriff questioningly, and Brandon nodded. The jailer dialled Carr's number, said after a few moments, "No one answers."

"Bunk!" Gregory said. "That's just a stall that you use on the suckers. The guys out here in the sticks may fall for that, but you can't get away with that stuff with someone who knows his way around. You just have some number that you know won't answer, and dial that whenever a sucker wants to communicate with a lawyer."

"Dial it yourself," the sheriff said.

Gregory advanced to the telephone.

"Just a minute," Selby warned. "Let's make sure that's the number he dials."

They watched him while he dialled Carr's number, watched the expression on his face as he realized the call was going to be unanswered. He waited almost thirty seconds before reluctantly dropping the receiver back into its cradle.

"Let him try again in about an hour," Brandon said to the jailer, then turned to the prisoner. "That's all, Gregory. You can try him again in an hour. In the meantime, go on into your cell."

Gregory stood sullenly defiant.

The jailer moved ominously forward. "You heard him, buddy," he said.

As Gregory still hesitated, the jailer went on scornfully, "And *you're* supposed to be a wise one! Smart guy, eh? You look down on the hicks, huh? Well, buddy, when you get back in circulation, just ask some of the boys who know about the guy that gets in jail and doesn't do what they tell him to. *There's* the sucker for you!"

The jailer slipped a swift wink at Sheriff Brandon, opened a drawer in the desk, ostentatiously took out a black-jack, slipped the leather thong around his wrist, and moved ominously toward Milton Gregory. "The sheriff said you were to go to your cell."

"All right, all right," Gregory said hastily. "Just show me where it is."

CHAPTER FIFTEEN

Brandon and Selby left the jail. Sylvia Martin was waiting in the car. "You're late for your appointment with Inez, Doug."

"I know it," Selby said, "but it couldn't be helped."

"Well," Sylvia Martin said cheerfully, "this is where I check out. I have a story to write, and I'll see you after you've called on her ... You can drop me off as you go by the office, Sheriff."

Brandon nodded.

The rain was still coming down in a cold fine spray composed of drops so small they hardly seemed more than mist; but those small drops were deceptive, and the felt hats of the county officials were soggy with moisture.

They dropped Sylvia off at *The Clarion* office, drove around to the apartment house where Inez Stapleton lived.

"How you going to explain the dog?" Brandon asked as he saw Selby preparing to take Fido in with him.

"Not going to. Just take him along as though he belonged to me."

He pushed the little black dog under his coat, and, with the sheriff, crossed the wet sidewalk, rang the bell of Inez Stapleton's apartment.

Almost immediately the electric buzzer released the door catch, and Selby and the sheriff entered.

"Third floor, isn't it?" the sheriff asked.

"That's right – 302; one of the front apartments."

They were whisked upward in the automatic elevator, walked back down the corridor toward the front of the building. Inez Stapleton stood in the doorway, framed against the subdued light of the cosy apartment. Selby's glance went first to the soft red wool jersey dress and then followed the graceful outlines of her tail, slender figure.

"You're late," she said.

"Couldn't help it," Selby said. "We had to go over across the river on some business, and then picked up a prisoner with whom we had a little trouble."

"My, but you're busy men," she laughed. "Come on in … Seems as though we manage to scare up quite a bit of crime for a rural community, doesn't it?"

"We have our share," the sheriff admitted.

There was a big fireplace at the north end of the apartment, and Inez had a cheerful, crackling wood fire going in the grate.

"Let me have your coats and hats," she said. "My, you certainly *do* get wet! I suppose you consider it's effeminate to carry umbrellas."

"They're always in the way," Selby explained.

"Never carried one in my life," Brandon announced.

"Why, Doug! What *have* you got? A dog! A little doggy! How cute! Hello, pooch. Are you vicious?"

She held the tips of her fingers to Fido's nose. Fido smelled tentatively, then wagged his tail.

"He's a friendly little cuss," Selby said.

"I didn't know you had a dog."

"I haven't had him long."

"What a cute pup!"

Selby put the dog down on the floor, said, "Make yourself at home, Fido," and to Inez, "I think you'll find him a perfect gentleman."

Fido walked over toward the fireplace, suddenly stopped, sniffed, moved over to one of the big chairs, and began violently wagging his tail.

"What is it, Fido?" Selby asked.

The dog barked.

"He's glad to be here," Inez said.

Selby glanced significantly at Brandon. "Seen your client tonight?" he asked Inez Stapleton.

"Why, yes. As it happens, she just left."

Once more Selby glanced at Brandon.

"I want to talk with her," Selby said.

"Well, it's – We'll talk it over. Sit down. Make yourselves comfortable there by the fire."

There was a certain homey comfort about the apartment. Selby was impressed by it. The warm cheerfulness, the evidences of the feminine touch here and there, contrasted with the cold, bleak, rainy night, contrasted even with Selby's own apartment which was little more than a place to sleep and read.

The young district attorney settled down in the chair by the fire with a sigh of solid comfort. The men extended their feet to the blaze, and the bottoms of their trousers began to give forth little wisps of steam.

There was something about Inez, Selby realized, that was thoroughly feminine. She might have her career as a lawyer during the daytime, but night would always find her in a *home*, a graciously attractive woman, poised, thoughtful, and beautiful.

Inez said gaily, "I splurged and made some coffee. Would you like some?"

Brandon looked at her. "Inez," he said, "you are more than intelligent. You're clairvoyant."

She laughed, but her eyes were anxiously fixed on Selby. "How about it, Doug?"

"I'd love it," Selby said, "if you think your ration card can stand such extravagances."

Inez looked wistful. "I don't have the opportunity very often, you know, Doug."

She moved toward the little kitchen. Brandon stretched out, flexing his muscles in the warmth of the fire. Then, as he heard Inez clattering cups and saucers in the kitchen, he leaned over to Doug, and said, "It's the woman's dog, all right. She was sitting in that chair. Notice the way the dog acted?"

Selby nodded.

Brandon said, "I can tell you something else. The woman isn't too good to that dog. The dog was glad to find she'd been here, but didn't try to follow the scent. Just seemed casually interested. She can't have been very kind to it."

Selby said, "One other explanation, Rex."

"What?"

"She may not have had the dog long, not over a week or ten days."

"*That*'s a thought," Brandon agreed.

Inez came into the room carrying a tray with two steaming cups of rich coffee, a pitcher of cream, and a bowl filled with sugar.

"No restrictions on this sugar," she said. "Use all you want."

Both of the men took cream, and sugar in their coffee, and, as they settled back to the enjoyment of it, soaked up the cosy warmth of the apartment. There was a gleam of quiet satisfaction in Inez Stapleton's eyes – eyes that almost never left Doug Selby's face.

She lit a cigarette, and sat down beside Doug's chair. "Doug, your feet are wet."

"Oh, just on the outside," he said.

"Nonsense, your feet are *soaked*. You should wear rubbers."

"I can't be bothered taking them off and putting them on."

"You should wear some heavier shoes then. You must have been walking around quite a bit."

"Oh, just a little – a few steps here and a few steps there. They all mount up. Inez, when can I interview Mrs Carleton Grines?"

"What about?"

"I want to ask her some questions."

"Can you tell me what they are?"

Selby hesitated thoughtfully, said, "Not very well."

"You're going to think I'm trying to pull a fast one, Doug, but I'm not."

"What do you mean?"

"You can't see her."

Selby lowered his coffee cup, looked up in surprise. "What's the idea?"

Inez said, "She's having, quote, a nervous breakdown, unquote."

"May I ask why?"

"You mean what brought it on?"

"Well, it probably amounts to the same thing."

"I know," she said, smiling, "but my way sounds better."

"All right," Selby asked, "what brought it on?"

"A gentleman by the name of A B Carr."

"He's rather ubiquitous," Selby said.

"Isn't he?"

Brandon started to say something, then changed his mind, and sipped his coffee instead.

Inez said, "I'm going to warm up that coffee a bit. Can't waste a drop, you know."

She went to the kitchen, returned with a silver coffeepot, poured hot coffee into their cups, then went back to the kitchen. When she returned, she said, "Doug, I don't know what to do with A B Carr."

"What's the matter with him?"

"He's representing Pervis Grines."

"You certainly keep abreast of the situation," Selby said.

"Don't I?"

"May I ask how you heard that?"

"Why?"

"The deal was only closed an hour or so ago."

She said, "I know it because Carr told me so."

"When?"

"About thirty minutes ago, here in this apartment."

"Make you a compromise offer?" Selby asked.

"You might call it that. He wants the lion's share for himself and his client. He'll condescend to let my client have twenty-five per cent."

"And did that give her, quote, a nervous breakdown, unquote?"

"No," Inez said. "Her, quote, nervous breakdown, unquote, came when she learned that Carr wanted to take her deposition. I thought that Carr had set the stage very nicely for these, quote, nervous breakdowns, unquote."

"How did he take the poor health of your client?"

"With very poor grace," she said. "Old ABC doesn't like it when you turn the tables on him. I explained to him very gravely that my client was in no condition to be questioned, that she was fully as upset as Carmen Freelman had been, and that I thought she should have the same treatment: seclusion in a sanitarium where she couldn't be disturbed."

"What did he say?"

"He got mad and started making threats."

"What sort of threats?"

"Oh, I don't know. He may have been just trying to frighten a young lawyer. You can't tell just what he *was* trying to do."

"But he made threats?"

"Well, the gist of his conversation seems to be that during the last ten years my client has not comported herself as a loyal wife, nor as a self-respecting widow. He's rather vague about it, but he intimates that a staff of private detectives could uncover things in her past life which would make cross-examination quite an ordeal."

"And so he wanted to take her deposition to give her a foretaste of it?"

"No," Inez said. "I knew exactly what he wanted to gain by that deposition. He wanted to be very suave and courteous, but ask her where she was in 1932, where she was 1933, where she was in 1934, and right on down the line; get all the addresses, where she was working, what she was doing, and all that. Then he'll be able to put private detectives on her trail and uncover – well, I don't know just what he would uncover."

"But you think it would be something?" Selby asked, smiling.

"I suppose he'll doubtless be able to find something he can twist and distort and use to worry the girl. That's because her relationship is that of a wife. On the other hand, his client is a brother, so it wouldn't do me any good to strike back at him that way … I think it's unfair. I think it's a dirty, contemptible way of trying to frighten my client out of her just property rights … Well, anyway, I looked him straight in the eyes and told him that it was unfortunate, that my client had suffered a shock of almost exactly the same nature as that suffered by Carmen Freelman, that he understood the effect of that shock on Carmen Freelman, that he himself had been the one who suggested she should go to the sanitarium where she couldn't be questioned, that Mrs Freelman had recovered after a few days and had returned of her own accord. I told him that I only hoped my client would make as rapid a recovery, but that, somehow, I didn't want to encourage him by holding out that hope, because I thought she would be rather slow in recuperating."

Selby grinned.

Brandon laughed outright. "I'd have given four bits to have been a fly on the wall and watched him then," he said. "What did he do?"

"His face got positively scarlet," Inez said. "He told me that he'd get an order of court forcing me to let his physician examine my client and make a report on her condition to the court."

"What did you say to that?" Selby asked.

"I told him that would be quite all right, that I'd ask the court to specify in the order that the same doctor who had examined Carmen Freelman, and decided that she should be kept free from all nerve strain, should be appointed to examine my client, and that he would be requested to specify in a written report to the court in exactly what particulars the condition of my client differed from that of Carmen Freelman."

"Then what?" Selby asked.

"He left shortly after that."

"All right," Selby said, "that's a nice bit of poetic justice for you to turn against Carr, but I want to examine your client."

"I'm sorry, Doug. It can't be done. If you questioned her, Carr would be entitled to question her. I'm not going to let her submit to that unless I have to. As a matter of fact, she has been through a good deal. She's had a nervous shock and an emotional upset. I have two doctors who will so testify. In fact, before any of this came up, one of them had been prescribing sleeping medicine for her and telling her to try to relax."

Selby said, "I'm not exactly in the same position Carr is. He is more or less powerless until he can get an order of the court. I am not."

"It's like we were telling someone else a little while ago," Brandon interjected. "There's easy ways of getting questions answered, and there's hard ways."

Inez blinked her eyes rapidly, but her chin was firm and determined. "I'm sorry," she said. "As far as I'm concerned, you're going to have to do it the hard way. I'm going to keep Mrs Carleton Grines out of circulation."

"May I ask why?" Selby asked.

"I told you. She's upset."

"Is it because some phase of her story doesn't agree with the facts?"

"Certainly not. If that were the case, I wouldn't continue to represent her ... I'm sorry, Doug. That's final, absolutely, positively final."

Selby finished his coffee, waited until Brandon returned the empty cup to the saucer.

"Well," he said, "just so we won't have any misunderstandings, remember that I warned you. I told you I was going to interview her."

"I know, Doug, but I think you'll appreciate my position."

Selby yawned, stretched, got up, said to Brandon, "Well, come on, Rex. Let's get going."

Brandon fingered the handle of his empty coffee cup solicitously.

"No, you don't," Selby said. "We get out of here and go to work. You'd settle down in front of this fire, and, by one excuse or another, would stay here just as long as Inez kept pouring the coffee."

"I still have a little left," she said.

"Get thee behind me, Satan. Come on, Rex. Let's get going ... And thanks for the hospitality, Inez."

Brandon said, "Just another five minutes wouldn't – "

Selby's eyes were level-lidded with hard significance. "Come on, Brandon."

Brandon caught that gaze, the subtle note in the tone, and was on his feet in a split instant. "Let's go," he said.

It wasn't until they were out in the hallway that Brandon ventured a comment. "I didn't get it at first, Doug. Why the hurry?"

Selby said, "Mrs Grines was in that room after Carr left. Carr left there about half an hour ago. Inez has to get some physician's certificates. That means as soon as she gets rid of us, she'll have doctors look Mrs Grines over. Inez wouldn't give us a break, so we're not going to give her one. We'll put a shadow on the doctors she's going to call. It's a cinch one of them is Dr Wilson. He likes Inez and would do anything within reason for her. We'll just watch where Dr Wilson goes and while he's in the middle of examining his patient, we'll drop in on the party."

Brandon said, "Hot dog! *That's* an idea."

Selby piloted him toward a public telephone booth. "All right, Rex, go ahead and call the office."

Brandon called the courthouse, left instructions for a deputy to get on the job and shadow the doctor, then came back to join Doug.

"Now what?" he asked.

Selby said, "We may as well take the dog back to Perkins, and leave him there until we locate Mrs Grines. Then we'll take her up to my office and arrange with Perkins to bring the dog in with him quite casually."

"Wait until tomorrow?" Brandon asked.

Selby shook his head. "I don't think so. Too many things are happening. Tomorrow may be too late ... Tell you what let's do, Rex. Let's pick up Sylvia Martin and go call on Carr. We can arrange with your office to telephone us just as soon as we locate Mrs Grines."

"Okay ... Doggone, but that was some of the best coffee I've ever tasted. Certainly did hit the spot."

"Uh huh," Selby said.

"I'll bet Carr had a fit when she pulled that nervous breakdown business on him ... Well, let's drive by and pick up Sylvia. We may as well give her a chance to be in on this, and when we get that call, things will move too fast for us to stop and pick her up."

Selby nodded.

The car ran slowly, the windshield wipers clicking crescents of clear vision on the windshield, the tyres hissing moisture in little streamlets thrown out on each side of the wheels.

"Seems like the rain's freshening a bit," Brandon said.

"I think the drops are getting a little larger," Selby replied in the voice of one who is thinking of something else.

"Nice to have a rain that soaks in this way early in the season. Do a lot of good. It's a pretty cold rain though. It won't bring out much feed in the hills unless there's a spell of warm weather, and that ain't likely. Haven't had much east wind this year."

"We haven't for a fact."

Brandon pulled the car into the kerb at *The Clarion* office. "Well, here we are."

Selby opened the door. "I'll run in and – "

The door of *The Clarion* building opened. Sylvia Martin signalled them.

"Good girl," Brandon said. "She's been working, but keeping an eye on the street so we wouldn't have to get out in the rain."

"It certainly helps a lot having her and *The Clarion* in our corner," Selby said.

"How's the dog doing?" Brandon asked.

Selby looked over to the back seat. "Sleeping."

"He's the sleepingest dog, isn't he?" Brandon laughed.

"Uh huh. Gets in an automobile, curls up, and goes to sleep. Seems crazy to get in the car, and then doesn't seem to pay too much attention to where he's going … You know, Rex, there's one thing about this case that bothers me."

"What is it?" Brandon asked.

Selby said, "We're being influenced an awful lot by the build-up."

"What do you mean?"

Before Selby could answer, Sylvia Martin came running across the sidewalk. Selby held the door open for her. Sylvia jumped in and said anxiously, "What luck?"

Selby said, "We think we've located the owner of the dog."

"Who?"

"Mrs Carleton Grines."

"Oh oh."

Brandon said, "And Doug was just about to give me some theory. What is it, Doug? What's this about the build-up?"

Selby said, "I've been unusually credulous. We all have. You know we sometimes take things for granted because of what is known as the build-up."

"What's the build-up in this thing, Doug?" the sheriff asked.

Selby said, "Suppose you picked up a criminal who was wanted by the police for a jail break among other things, and he told you that he really didn't know who he was; that from the very moment he escaped jail he had been suffering from amnesia and that he simply couldn't recall a thing that had happened before his arrest? – What would you say to that?"

Brandon grinned, then looked serious. "I'd say it was just the same old stall that they all use."

"Exactly," Selby agreed, "but because the man has made some money, because the story comes to us in a lot of repetitions, we take it at its face value. Gillespie, for instance, doesn't *know* anything about Billmeyer's loss of memory, except what Billmeyer told him. The same is true of Carmen. The same of Billmeyer's wife. We've acted on the assumption that Billmeyer received a jolt which made him suddenly remember his past life, that he went to the place where his clothes had been stored for ten years, and found them, that he couldn't have had prior access to those clothes because the envelope in the pocket would have told him who he was … But suppose that amnesia business is simply the subterfuge of a clever crook? Then what?"

"Well," Sylvia asked excitedly, "what then? Go on with it, Doug."

"Then," Selby said, "the tweed suit takes on a very sinister aspect."

"I don't get you, Doug. If the amnesia was a fake, he'd have had the suit of clothes hanging in his closet, could have gone and got it whenever he wanted."

Selby shook his head vehemently. "That suit of clothes with the letter in the pocket would have been the last thing on earth he'd ever have kept in his closet. That letter itself – or rather the envelope – is a most incriminating piece of evidence. He'd never have kept it where a janitor, housekeeper, or servant could have found it. He'd never have kept it at all. The first thing Billmeyer would have done would have been to have destroyed that suit of clothes, and particularly the envelope."

Brandon said, "By George, you're right!"

"Then where did the tweed suit come from?" Sylvia asked.

Selby said, "That's a question. It isn't a simple question. If Billmeyer didn't have that suit, who *did* have it?"

"Brings us right back to the wife every time," Brandon said.

Selby nodded. "Now, let's suppose the wife had the suit. Her husband had apparently died in a jail break. She kept the suit for ten years … That doesn't sound logical, does it?"

"No."

"The only thing that would make her keep the suit," Selby went on, "is that she had a pretty shrewd suspicion her husband was alive, had deliberately chosen not to communicate with her because he was afraid to do so, but she expected him to show up at any moment, so she kept his suit of clothes."

"For ten years?" Brandon asked dubiously.

"Yes, she would," Sylvia Martin said. "After she once started keeping it, she'd keep right on. In other words, it's so gradual.

You can't say, 'Well, I'm going to throw that suit of clothes away tomorrow, or next week, or next month.' You keep it … And, as I understand it, this suit had been kept in a camphorwood chest. Isn't that right, Doug?"

"Apparently so. There's an odour of camphor about it – different from moth balls."

"Well, there you are," Sylvia said. "The suit was put away … You're right again, Doug. Only a wife would have done it just that way."

Selby said, "Let's not get too far ahead of ourselves, but it's a possibility to take into consideration. Dog hairs on the suit, and the dog getting excited up in Inez Stapleton's apartment. It begins to make a pattern … We're on our way to call on Old ABC, Sylvia. Thought you might like to come along."

"Anything in particular?" she asked.

"No. We're just going to pay our respects, and, in case he doesn't know it, tell him his client's in jail, and see what he says."

Sylvia said, "Somehow, I'm afraid of him, Doug. He's tricky, and he's dangerous. He wouldn't be above framing you in some kind of a political deal."

"I know it," Selby agreed.

"He associates with all sorts of crooks who would be willing to swear to anything – or, as far as that's concerned, to *do* anything – the minute old Maestro crooked his finger at them."

"It's unfortunate that he had to bring that atmosphere of city gangdom to Madison City," Selby admitted, "but we're not going to conform to *his* ways. He's going to conform to *ours*. Let's go, Rex."

CHAPTER SIXTEEN

The county car slid away from the kerb, swished through the rain, climbed the long grade up to Orange Heights, and sloshed along the wet pavement until it came to the big house Carr had purchased. It was a huge, Spanish-style structure with white stucco walls, a red tile roof, and red tile projections over the doors and windows with, here and there, convenient balconies with wrought-iron railings.

"Doesn't look as though anyone's home," Brandon said.

Sylvia exclaimed, "I see a light!"

"Where?" Brandon asked.

"Just a glimpse of illumination that I caught for a minute coming past the drapes about midway along the side of the house. I guess it's the library. Looked as though someone had been standing at the window with the drapes in back of him shutting off the illumination, and then suddenly stepped back into a room."

"Well," Selby said, "we'll soon find out."

Brandon parked the car in front of the house.

"How about the pooch, Doug?"

Selby surveyed the sleeping dog. "Let him stay here. We'll roll down the windows part way so he can get plenty of air – not far enough to let in the rain."

They rolled down the windows of the car, the fine, misting rain striking the edges of the glass and spattering into a cold spray.

Selby said, "I'm afraid that's going to get the cushions wet. Tell you what we'll do, Rex. Roll the windows all the way *up* on the windward side and all the way *down* on the lee side."

"Don't think he'll get out?" Brandon asked.

"Apparently, he's more inclined to get in than to get out. Anyway, he's sound asleep."

They emerged from the car, started up the walk which led to the front door, and had taken only a few steps when suddenly, as though by magic, lights came on all over the place. There were floodlights which illuminated the sides of the house, overhead lights which blazed down on the ground, lights which turned the driveway to the garage into white brilliance. All over the magnificent estate, so far as could be noticed, there was not a single shadow in which anyone could hide.

From the interior of the house they heard, faintly muffled, the sound of musical chimes.

"What the devil!" Brandon exclaimed, recoiling as though someone had shot at him.

Selby was interested, said, "Wait a minute. Let's try an experiment."

He took Sylvia Martin's arm with one hand, Brandon's with the other, piloted them back toward the automobile. At the second step the lights suddenly clicked off. Rain-filled darkness descended on the grounds, and, after the blazing brilliance of the floodlights, it seemed as though the whole house was shrouded in a thick smoke screen.

"All right," Selby said, "right about face. Here we go again."

They turned sharply, and, before they had gone four feet, the lights blazed on once more. Once again the musical chimes sounded from the inside of the house.

"Got it," Selby said. "He's got the grounds patrolled by beams of invisible light. As soon as anyone crosses one of those beams of light, it turns on all the floodlights and starts the chimes. I'd heard he was doing some electrical work out here, but didn't know exactly what it was."

Brandon said, "The thing's uncanny. He can do that with a beam of invisible light?"

"Sure," Selby said. "He probably has the whole ground crisscrossed with those beams so you can't approach the house from any direction without turning on all those floodlights."

They started toward the house once more.

Brandon said disgustedly, "An honest man doesn't need all that stuff. You mark my words. Some night we're going to be called out here because the neighbours heard a shot, and we'll find Old ABC has been the one on the receiving end. I don't care how carefully a man tries to guard himself, when he gets to the point that – "

The front door swung open. The tall figure of Carr stood on the threshold, his manner slightly sardonic, yet at the same time suave and smiling.

"Good evening. *Good* evening," he called. "Do come in, gentlemen. Don't stand there in the rain discussing my new gadgets. Come in and let me show you how they work ... Ah, Miss Martin of *The Clarion*. Well, *well*, this is indeed a pleasure. But *do* come in. It's a wet night, and you'll find the house nice and comfortable."

They trudged up to the porch.

"Rather ingenious, don't you think?" Carr asked.

"The lights?" Selby inquired.

"Yes."

"They seem to be quite effective."

"I can assure you they're *very* effective. Of course, I can't point out all the details because some of them are secret, but it's absolutely impossible for anyone to approach this house by any of the legitimate means of ingress without illuminating the entire place and sounding the chimes. And it's absolutely impossible for anyone to approach by what I might call the illegitimate means – such as detouring around over the lawn, or sneaking around behind the bushes – without having all the lights come on, having police whistles sound an alarm, and having concealed motion picture cameras automatically start grinding out photographs of the intruder. Rather a neat way to guard against unwelcome visitors, don't you think?"

Brandon grunted. "When I first came to this county," he said, "up in the mountains, no one even locked the doors. People were welcome to come in at any time. We always kept provisions on hand in the cabin, and dry firewood. If we didn't happen to be home, persons dropping in would cook themselves a meal – only thing was they was supposed to leave dry wood when they left."

"Most interesting," Carr said, "a very touching tribute to human nature … You were running a cattle ranch, I believe, Sheriff?"

"That's right."

"Most interesting. It bears out my contention that men who live in the open are more rugged and honest than those who spend their lives within cities; but we mustn't stand here talking while you're all wet. Take your things off. Here, let me hang them up. That's right … Rather an ingenious device, this. I put them right in this closet and touch this button."

Carr touched a little switch button, and instantly the closet was filled with a draft of warm air. There was a peculiar, deep-throated whirring sound.

"Powerful fan," Carr explained. "Circulates warm, drying air through that closet. You'll be surprised. In just a few minutes your things will be perfectly dry. Just a little touch, you know. The house is air conditioned, and it was very easy to install this drying device. Makes it rather convenient for visitors on a cold, wintry evening … But do come in and sit down. Here I am, standing here, showing you the little gadgets and being remiss in my hospitality."

Carr ushered them into the library, a sumptuously furnished room. Concealed lights in the wall furnished a flood of indirect illumination which gave plenty of light, yet seemed restful to the eyes. There were deep-cushioned chairs with footstools in front of them, tables at the side with smoking things conveniently to hand. The walls of the room were lined with well-filled bookcases, and there was that about the books which indicated they were really read and enjoyed and were not just for purposes of ornament. Moreover, the room had that peculiar atmosphere of cosy utility so seldom found in large rooms, and never found in rooms which are not actually lived in.

Carr saw that they were comfortably seated, passed cigars and cigarettes, then pressed a button.

A white-coated Filipino, a man nearing middle age, small, slender, quick in his motions, and with alert eyes, stood in the doorway as though he had been standing only a step or two away merely waiting for the sound of the bell.

Carr said, "I think Salvio is new since you were here last, Selby. He's a very valuable addition – interesting history. Falsely accused of poisoning his common-law wife, a very attractive blonde. Had one hung jury, and then I secured an acquittal on the retrial ... Now what will you have? Let me suggest hot buttered rum, or Salvio can make a very excellent Tom and Jerry ... Or perhaps just a hot eggnog?"

Selby smiled and shook his head. "This is an official visit, Carr."

"Come, come," Carr said. "That won't interfere with just a little drink."

"I'm afraid it will."

"But surely Miss Martin is not on business. I can order you something to ward off the bad after-effects of a wetting, Miss Martin?"

Sylvia smiled her thanks but also shook her head.

"And I can't tempt you, Sheriff?"

"No, thanks," Brandon said shortly.

Carr wagged his head from side to side, professing to be very much surprised. "When you people are on duty, you certainly *are* abstemious! I've never seen anything like it. Why, gentlemen, up in the city, when an officer calls on you he won't even put the handcuffs on until after you've bought him a couple of drinks."

Selby laughed outright. Brandon didn't even smile.

Carr turned to the houseboy. "Nothing."

"Don't let us stop you," Selby said.

Carr smiled. "There is no pleasure in drinking alone, and I'm afraid it would be a refined torture for you to see me sipping a hot buttered rum ... No, gentlemen, I, too, will share the inconvenience caused by your official duties ... By the way, Selby, I must congratulate you. It was splendid, absolutely magnificent. But why in the world didn't you take the credit for it?"

"Credit for what?" Selby asked.

"Putting me out of the running, switching those automobiles around so that I inadvertently stole yours. You would have died laughing if you could have been along and seen the aftermath of your little sleight-of-hand. I was so mad at those thick-skulled radio police. I told them I was driving the car I had rented, that they had made a mistake in copying off the numbers of the car that had been stolen."

Carr broke off his recital to laugh heartily at the recollection of his own predicament.

"What happened?" Selby asked curiously.

"Oh," Carr said, "I led with my chin all the way along the line. I raved and I ranted. I went down to police headquarters – unwillingly, of course. Once there, I knew that it was too late to do anything except vindicate myself and perhaps lay the foundation for a damage suit against the city. So I ran the thing down. I insisted on seeing the numbers which had been taken down over the telephone at the police department. Then I thought the man at the rental agency had made a mistake and confused numbers in making out the cards of the automobile, so I insisted on taking a couple of officers out to the rental agency … Well, of course, you know the answer."

Selby said, "I'm sorry I had to do it."

"Sorry!" Carr exclaimed. "Good heavens, Counsellor, you aren't joking?"

"No," Selby said shortly, "I mean it. It was a bit of trickery."

"Marvellous trickery!" Carr exclaimed. "You slipped one over on Old ABC, and there's many a district attorney who would like to clasp your hand in congratulation."

Sylvia Martin, noticing Doug's embarrassment, said, "Why not let the rest of us in on it, Mr Carr?"

"Good heavens, hasn't Selby told *you!*"

She shook her head.

Carr seemed at a loss for a moment, then said, "Yes, I can understand that. You'd have published it if he'd told you. The fact that you haven't published it shows you didn't know … Well, I'll give you the facts. It's one on me. I should really shave my head in penance."

Selby tried to interrupt but Carr proceeded with the story of the District Attorney's visit to the sanitarium in all its detail.

Sylvia Martin stared at Doug with eyes that were wide with astonished incredulity. "Doug, you mean she didn't return of her own volition, that you – "

"No, certainly she came back of her own volition," Selby said somewhat stiffly.

"After you'd talked to her!"

"Well, yes."

Sylvia Martin said indignantly, "And you kept this quiet, let *The Blade* lambaste you for letting Carmen Freelman slip through your fingers, and then never took credit for any of this, let the people think Carmen Freelman simply came back entirely of her own accord?"

Selby said, "Frankly, I'm ashamed of the whole business. It was a trick, and I'm sorry that I had to do it."

Carr's face showed his emotions. "He means it! Such naïveté! Such modesty! And such damnable ingenuity! Do you know, Selby, there are times when I find I'm becoming just a little afraid of you? But don't worry, Miss Martin, about the publicity angle."

"I'm not," Sylvia Martin said grimly. "Wait until I write this up."

"Go right ahead," Carr said. "The more the merrier. Joseph Bagley Raft is going to make quite a feature story of it in the metropolitan press ... Do you know Raft?"

"I know of him," Sylvia said cautiously.

"A very good friend of mine," Carr said. "Many a time I've given him a tip that has resulted in his bringing home the bacon with a startling story. I was telling Joe Raft about this, and he doubled up with laughter, said that he was going to publish it as a feature story entitled *Man Bites Dog*. I – " Carr broke off to listen as a telephone rang; then, as they heard Salvio answering it, Carr went on, "it's not exactly the type of publicity I want, but then, after all, it's publicity. Keeps my name before the public, and you can gamble that Joe Raft won't let me down on it. He'll make it appear that it was the exception that proves the rule, if you get what I mean ... A friendly press is a great asset – "

Carr broke off as Salvio appeared silently in the doorway and nodded.

"Important?" Carr asked.

"I think quite important."

Carr said, "Excuse me a moment, please."

Sylvia said to Doug Selby as Carr left the room, "I could bump you for not telling me about that, Doug."

Selby said uncomfortably, "It wouldn't have been fair to Carmen Freelman – and it *was* a bit of trickery."

"Bah!" Sylvia exclaimed. "As far as Carmen Freelman is concerned, I don't think she's entitled to any consideration, and as far as the trickery is concerned, you were dealing with Old ABC. You were dealing with a man who had tried to trick you into a disadvantageous position. He'd whisked the witness out of your hands and was laughing at you. Then he'd bribed the sanitarium – Trickery, my eye. It was just getting even with him."

Brandon said, "I'd have given five bucks to have been there and seen it."

Sylvia laughed. "If you'd been there, you wouldn't have seen it," she said.

"What do you mean?"

Sylvia said, "About the time Carr stood up there in the sanitarium and started manipulating things so you couldn't get in to see Mrs Freelman, you'd have eliminated Mr Carr from the scenery with one very good right-hand punch."

Brandon doubled his right fist, stroked the knuckles with the fingers of his left hand, grinned, and said, "Now *that's* an idea."

Carr re-entered the room, his manner still suave, but he was no longer smiling. "I understand," he said, "that you have another client of mine in your hostelry, Sheriff."

"Milton Gregory?" Selby asked.

"Yes."

"I was going to tell you about him," Selby said.

Carr resumed his chair. "At times, Selby, I find you very annoying – in your official capacity, of course. As an individual, I find you charming."

Selby said, "The reason for our visit was to talk with you about Milton Gregory."

"Indeed?"

"Yes. You said you were representing his sister."

"Did I?"

Selby thought back over the conversation, frowned, and said, "You came to my office with Milton Gregory. You explained to me that his sister had had a nervous breakdown. You tried to keep Milton Gregory from doing any talking."

Carr positively beamed. "That's absolutely correct, Counsellor."

Selby said, "I am under the impression that you mentioned Carmen Freelman had retained you. In any event, you *didn't* tell me that Milton Gregory was your client in another matter."

"Tut tut, Counsellor, I can't be responsible for your understanding of my conversation. I mentioned in so many words that I was doing the talking for Milton Gregory."

"But you didn't mention that he was your client."

"And am I supposed to hand you a list of my clients simply because you're district attorney?"

Brandon said bluntly, "I think we've had enough of this, Carr. We want to know why young Gregory employed you."

Carr's smile was urbane. "Well now, Sheriff, it's unfortunate that I can't answer that question. An attorney, you understand, isn't supposed to talk about the affairs of his client. The law protects that relationship. Not only am I not supposed to talk about them, but no power on earth can make me. And that, in case you're interested, is the law."

Selby said, "You were calling on Pervis Grines tonight."

"Well, well, *well!* You certainly *do* get around!" Carr laughed. "That's one thing I can't get accustomed to, Selby. Living in a small community where everyone knows every time you turn around."

"What," Brandon asked, "did you go over there for?"

Carr smiled again. "I'm sorry to have to keep refusing to answer your questions, Sheriff. Not that I think my affairs are any of your damn business, but I dislike to be put in the position of seeming inhospitable. If I were in your office and you asked me the question, I'd tell you to go jump in the lake, but being here in my house, where you are, for the moment, my guest, you embarrass me, Sheriff."

Brandon's face flushed. Selby found himself smiling.

There was a moment's silence; then Selby said, "Carr, I'm going to ask you a question. It's a pertinent question. I want an answer to it."

"Well, let's have a look at the question, Counsellor."

"When Carleton Grines or Desmond Billmeyer, whichever you want to call him, was found dead at the foot of the grade, half in and half out of that stolen sedan, he was wearing a suit of tweeds. That suit of tweeds didn't fit him very well. It was a suit he had last worn, so far as we know, some ten years ago when he left Oklahoma. I want to know, Carr, if you know anything about that suit of clothes, anything at all."

Carr hesitated. "As far as I know," he said, in the cautious manner of one choosing his words, "I never saw it before."

"And you know nothing about it?"

"Let me put it this way, Selby. Of my own knowledge, I know nothing whatever about that suit of clothes. I might make certain deductions. Doubtless, I have made those deductions, but I have no actual knowledge. In other words, I would not be a witness."

"All right," Brandon said, "what are your deductions?"

Carr smiled at him again. "Sheriff, you're going to have to let me buy you a drink, or make you a sandwich, or do something to show you that I'm not entirely inhospitable."

"Meaning you aren't going to answer that question?" Brandon asked.

"Precisely, Sheriff. My deductions are purely the result of my own thought processes, and I use them to better my financial position. In other words, I make my living by using my brain, and I don't intend to give away any of my stock in trade."

"If you have some ideas about that suit of clothes, you should give them to us," Brandon insisted doggedly.

"Good heavens, Sheriff, why?"

"It might help us determine who committed the murder, for one thing."

"You're absolutely right, Sheriff. It might. I'm forced to agree with you there. I'm glad you mentioned it, because it's very embarrassing to find myself disagreeing with you all the time."

"All right," Brandon said, "go ahead. Keep pulling that sardonic line if you get any pleasure out of it. I'm talking facts."

"And *I'm* trying to talk facts, as you so bluntly express it, Sheriff."

"All right, why won't you tell us what your deductions are if they don't tend to prove the guilt of your client?"

"Well now," Carr said, positively beaming at the irate sheriff, "that's a point, Sheriff. You see I make my living, as I have explained to you, out of selling my thoughts. If Madison County had employed me to act as its attorney, I'd give it the benefit of my cerebration. Your young friend over there, the district attorney, *has* been employed by the county, and he certainly is loyal to his employer. He's giving dear old Madison County everything he has.

"But you see, Sheriff, they haven't seen fit to employ me. Therefore, I make certain deductions, and by acting upon those deductions I feather my financial nest."

"Meaning you know who the murderer is?" Selby asked.

"Well now, Counsellor, I wouldn't go so far as to say that, but I have certain theories which are most intriguing. I want to investigate them. It is quite possible that I *may* find out who committed the murder, and if I do, you can rest assured that I will try, insofar as is in my power, to make that information bring me some financial return … Tut tut, now, Sheriff," Carr said hastily, holding up his hand as Brandon started to say something. "Let me finish, please. I was going to say that I would try to use the information to feather my financial nest as well as I could and *still be within the law*. I wouldn't compound a felony, of course, and I wouldn't resort to what is popularly known as blackmail. But I don't think I would become unduly patriotic and write a letter to the paper which employs the charming Miss Martin, and say, 'Dear Editor: I think so-and-so committed the murder for the following reasons,' and sign it, *Pro Bono Publico*."

Selby got to his feet. "Well," he said, "under the circumstances, we won't take up any more of your time, Carr."

The triumphant gleam left Carr's eyes. He quit his mental sparring with the sheriff, turned thoughtful eyes on Selby. "No, don't go," he said. "I want to talk with you about Milton Gregory."

"What about him?" Selby asked, still standing.

"What do you propose to do with him?"

Selby's smile just missed being a grin, "Well now, Carr," he said, "as you as aptly expressed it, I'm being employed by Madison County, and, in my own small way, I make certain deductions. And since you're not giving Madison County the benefit of your deductions, I'm quite certain that Madison County wouldn't want me to give you the benefit of mine."

Carr's voice lost its banter as the others got up from their chairs. "You can't stall me off this way, Selby. I want to know just what the charge is against Milton Gregory and what you propose to do with him."

"Yes," Selby said, "I gathered that you wished that information. You conveyed that idea – at least to me. How about you, Sheriff? Didn't you gather from Carr's conversation that was what he wanted?"

Carr, suddenly angry, took a quick step forward. Sheriff Brandon's broad shoulders pivoted as he stepped between the criminal lawyer and the district attorney.

Then suddenly Carr laughed. "Selby, you really *are* clever. I have to hand it to you. Here I have been – well, rubbing it in on the sheriff a little, if you like. And now, when it comes to something where you have the whip hand, you turn my own weapon right back at me. Gentlemen, I apologize. I brought it on myself. I have no kick coming. And yet I became angry for the moment. The reason I'm a poor loser is that I've never had much practice at it ... Well, gentlemen, I trust we understand each other. You aren't giving me any information, so I propose to set the machinery of the law to get the information I want from you."

"You're certainly entitled to do that," Selby said. "This is Saturday night. You might even get a judge to sign a writ of *habeas corpus* tomorrow. The writ would be returnable either Monday or Tuesday, probably Monday afternoon."

Carr frowned. "A lot can happen between now and Monday afternoon, Selby."

"It can indeed," Selby conceded. "I'm forced to agree with you, Carr, and, as you have so aptly pointed out when we have had adverse positions on so many occasions, it's a pleasure to find myself in accord with you."

Carr said, "Oh, damn! I should have known better than to have started that line with you. All right, Selby, we'll let it go at that. I've had my fun, and you've had yours. Now, we'll see what can be done. You can probably prevent me from knowing what you have up your sleeve until Monday or Tuesday. On the other hand, I can assure you you won't get anything out of Milton Gregory. You can't keep me from visiting my client in the jail, and after I've talked with him – well, you'll find a clam positively voluble compared with young Mr Gregory."

Selby, walking toward the front door, said, "That's quite all right, Carr, and, of course, if you don't get the writ of *habeas corpus* issued tomorrow, it's quite possible it will be Wednesday afternoon before you know what I intend to do with young Gregory."

Carr moved out into the hall, opened the door of the closet, said, "You're quite right, Counsellor. I can't quarrel with that statement … And here are your things, all nice and warm and dry … I'm afraid your feet are wet. I certainly hope you don't catch cold, and do come again. Please don't feel that you have to wait to call until some official business brings you here. I'd be only too glad to have you drop in any time, and if you could come when you didn't feel that your official duties made it necessary for you to be so damned abstemious, we could perhaps have a drink together."

"Thank you," Selby said, dryly.

Carr held the door open for them. "Well, good night. It's a cold, wet night. A nasty rain. Think it's coming down a little harder than it was an hour or so ago. And I suppose I'll have to go down to your jail in order to give young Mr Gregory proper instructions on what to say in case he's interrogated … You'll notice that my floodlighting system doesn't come on when guests are departing. That's because the floodlights would dazzle you, but the lights will automatically come on as you get past a certain point there in the walk. They will light you out toward your car – and assure me that you go directly to your car! Well, good night. Good night."

They trudged on down the walk, and, as Carr had promised, abruptly the floodlights clicked into brilliance, illuminating the grounds as though a vivid flash of lightning had been suddenly frozen into immobility.

"I don't like that man," Brandon said with feeling.

"He was trying to irritate you," Selby laughed, "and that's a good sign. That shows we're really getting under his skin. For some reason or other, arresting Milton Gregory was quite a blow to Carr."

"Perhaps it was a blow to his pride," Sylvia Martin said. "He'd taken such pains to hide Gregory, and then you put your finger on him so easily."

"Well," Selby said, "we're going to get hold of Mrs Carleton Grines, and then perhaps we'll know more."

They crossed what was evidently the release beam of invisible light, and every one of the floodlights going off at the same time made the night seem unusually dark.

Sylvia Martin said, "Doug, if you'd only given *me* the true story of Carmen Freelman's return! You just wait until I write that up. Even now, it isn't too late to do some good."

Selby held the car door open for Sylvia, climbed in after her. Brandon slid in behind the steering wheel, and started the motor throbbing. "It did me good," he said, "to hear Doug pour that stuff right back at Carr. Dammit, the man makes me mad. If he'd come right out and cuss me, and call me everything he could lay his tongue to, I wouldn't get half as mad as when he gets that patronizing air – "

"Well," Sylvia Martin said as the sheriff's voice trailed off into silence while he was turning the car, "Doug had – Doug, *where's* the dog?"

Selby whirled to look over at the back seat, then, groping for the switch, flashed on the dome light.

The back seat was entirely empty.

"He may have crawled down – No, he didn't either. He isn't in the car."

Brandon pulled in close to the kerb and slowed.

"Well," Selby said, "it looks as though Carr had the last laugh."

"You mean he's got the dog?"

"That telephone call," Selby said, "may have been prearranged. He probably gave that Filipino houseboy a signal to see that the telephone rang, and then call – "

"But he wasn't out of the room long enough to have gone out to the automobile," Sylvia said. "He was only gone a few seconds."

175

"Long enough," Selby pointed out, "to tell the houseboy to go out to the car and bring the dog in."

Brandon said, "That damn crooked lawyer! Now, what would *he* want with our dog?"

"The same thing *we* wanted with him," Selby said. "Carr's smart. Don't ever overlook that. Of course, Rex, there's a chance the dog got out under his own power."

"But why?" Brandon asked.

"Because he was home."

"You mean he was Carr's dog?"

"Either that or he lives in that neighbourhood, and has been around Carr's house … . Either of you remember ever having seen Carr with a dog?"

"Not me," Brandon said. "But I don't see him very often."

"I see him quite frequently," Sylvia said, "not to speak to, but driving around town. I can't ever remember having seen a dog with him."

"Then he wants the dog for the same thing we did," Brandon said. "He knows the dog's a clue."

"He's more than a clue," Selby pointed out. "He's actual evidence. The dog comes pretty close to being proof. Suppose Carr goes to call on Mrs Carleton Grines, takes the dog with him. The dog barks and yelps gleefully. Then Carr suavely points out that he didn't know that the dog was hers, that doubtless I'd like very much to establish that fact, and then suggests to her that she accept a very low compromise offer in connection with the estate and – Well, you can see what he's up to."

"That's *exactly* it," Sylvia Martin said.

Brandon started to turn the car. "All right," he said, "we'll go get that dog back. We – "

"Wait a minute, Rex," Selby said, putting a hand on the wheel.

"What's the matter?" the sheriff asked.

"You can't do it."

"The hell I can't."

"In the first place," Selby said, "Carr wouldn't let us search his house without a warrant. In the second place, if we did search it, it wouldn't do any good. If he sent that Filipino houseboy out to get the dog from our car, he certainly wasn't foolish enough to have the dog placed where he could be caught red-handed. No, Rex, we've got to play it another way. We've got to get to Mrs Grines first; then we've got to put a watch on Carr's house. The minute he leaves, an officer will stop him to check up on his car registration or his headlights or something of that sort. Then if the dog's in the automobile with him, we'll have Carr arrested for stealing the dog."

"And Carr will say that he found the dog somewhere on the highway, or that the dog came to his back door and whined, and he took him in."

"Oh, certainly," Selby said. "Carr will have an ingenious and plausible explanation, but the point is, *we'll* have the dog."

"But we can't do any good with Mrs Grines until we do have the dog," Brandon said.

Selby nodded. "I could kick myself for giving Carr that opportunity. The man's clever. You can see what happened. We went over to call on Pervis Grines. Grines saw the dog in the automobile when we went out, and after we'd left, he got to thinking perhaps they'd talked a little too much, so he rang up Old ABC. That may have been the call that came in while we were there … Tell you what you do, Rex. You and Sylvia wait here in the automobile. Switch out the lights and just sit here. I'll walk on down the hill, pick up my machine, telephone your office, and tell them to round up some deputy they can trust, and send him out here. But my best guess is Carr will come driving out within a matter of minutes."

"You can't do that, Doug," Sylvia said. "It's half a mile down there. In this rain – "

Selby opened the car door. "My feet are wet already. Walking will do me good. Stir up the circulation."

Sylvia, reaching a sudden decision, slid along the front seat, jumped to the ground. "All right, Doug, I'm coming with you."

"You can't, Sylvia. It's wet and rainy and – "

"And *my* feet are already wet, and *I* need exercise to warm up. Come on, Doug, let's go, and let Rex get back on the job."

Selby said, "All right, we haven't time to argue. Remember, Rex, the minute you see him come out of the driveway, stop him. Tell him his headlights are glaring. Go through every inch of his car. If you find the dog, drag him up to the office."

"Doug is right," Brandon said. "I'd just like to put that bird under arrest and have him resist."

Selby said, "I think we stand a good chance. He'll come out just as soon as he thinks the coast is clear. Come on, Sylvia. Let's go."

CHAPTER SEVENTEEN

They started walking down the sidewalk, the cold rain drizzling against their faces.

"Feels good, doesn't it?" Sylvia asked, swinging along at Selby's side.

"Uh huh. I like the feel of rain on my face."

"So do I."

"Your feet very wet?" Selby asked, solicitously.

"Sopping, but it doesn't make any difference. As long as I keep moving, I'm all right."

Selby walking along silently for a hundred yards, then said, "Some of these big houses up here are going to be quite a headache with the high income taxes."

"I've been wondering about that," she said.

"There's Gillespie's house over there," Selby said, indicating one of the spacious houses over on the left. "He's a widower. Lives there with three servants. The place must be quite an expense to keep up, to say nothing of depreciation and – "

"What is it?" she asked as Doug broke off abruptly.

"I've been wondering about that telephone call of Gillespie's."

"What about it?"

"Jason Gillespie called Billmeyer while Stephen Freelman was there at Gillespie's house. Remember? We have both the statement of Gillespie and that of Stephen for it."

"That's right."

"But Carmen Freelman says she met Billmeyer in Las Alidas. She couldn't have, not if Gillespie's call was to Hollywood."

Sylvia said, "Doug, that's frightfully important. If you could catch Carmen in another lie – "

Selby said, "Somehow, I don't think she's lying, but when you come right down to it, I don't think Gillespie ever stated definitely that he called Billmeyer in Hollywood – although he may have. That was the impression he gave me, but – I'm going to take a run over there and ask him, Sylvia."

"All right, I'll come along with you."

"No, there's no need. I'll sprint up the walk, just knock on the door, and ask him."

"Oh, nonsense. I'll come along. It'll only take a minute."

Selby said, "When you come right down to it, he – "

"What, Doug?"

"I've been doing a little thinking."

"What is it, Doug?"

Selby said abruptly, "You wait here. I'm just going to run across and ask Gillespie that one question."

Before she could move, Selby had jumped over the low cement coping and was streaking across the wet grass. He ran up on the porch and rang the bell.

The porch light came on almost instantly. A safety catch slipped off the door.

"Well, well, hello, Selby. Good heavens, you're wet. What's the matter? Car break down or something? Come on in."

Gillespie threw the door wide open.

Selby said, "I just wanted to ask one question about that telephone call you put through to Billmeyer on Thanksgiving. I won't come in. I'm all wet. I – "

From the interior of the house, Selby heard a whine, then a sharp bark. Claws scratched the waxed floor as Fido bounded around the corner and ran up to Selby.

Gillespie said, "Fido, get back. Why, you never acted like this before. Down, Fido. Come in, Selby."

Selby backed slowly away from the threshold. "I won't come in. I'm all wet. I – "

Cold, hard lights glinted in Gillespie's eyes. His hand moved out from his side. Selby saw the ominous glint of blued steel. "I said come in," Gillespie announced without raising his voice. "When I say come in, I mean it."

Selby walked toward him, pretending not to understand the significance of the gun. "Well, all right, I – "

Gillespie kept moving backward. A gust of rain-sodden wind sucked the front door shut with a slam.

Gillespie's eyes were like bits of cold steel on a frosty morning. "Don't try it, Selby," he warned. "Don't come any closer. I'm not going to try to bluff it out. You see, I've a death warrant on the tips of my fingers. Once you take my fingerprints, I'm done for. You're a shrewd one. You really are. But it wasn't the telephone call that trapped me. It was something else. It must have been the dog.

"No use in trying to conceal things from you now, Selby. I had my choice to make when that dog barked. I made it, with a six-gun to enforce my command. I never was one to hesitate when it came to a showdown, Selby.

"Fido must have jumped in the car with Billmeyer. Or perhaps some of Fido's hairs were on that suit I'd been keeping. I suppose a microscopic examination showed you the dog hairs. I noticed the place where a sharp pair of scissors had cut off a lock of Fido's hair. Been wondering about it. I'd been up at Miss Inez Stapleton's, and I thought perhaps you might have dropped in there and had the dog with you. He'd have caught my scent, and barked, perhaps – although he isn't very fond of me ... Rather clever bit of detective work, I should say, Selby, but it's not going to gain you anything."

Selby studied his chances, as a boxer studies his opponent in those first few seconds following the gong in the opening round. He saw nothing to reassure him. Gillespie's face was a mask of cold determination.

Gillespie seemed to read his thoughts. "Don't try it, Selby. We're at the end of the road, you and I. I don't want to kill you. I may have to do it. But one thing's certain: I won't be taken alive, and if I go, you're going with me. Not that I have anything against you. But right now you're my best life insurance."

Selby said, "I can't understand this. I thought you were Carleton Grines' best friend."

"I was. I was the one who smuggled the guns and saws into that Oregon jail. I had his clothes."

"And you killed him?"

"Technically, I killed him. But I didn't intend to. Poor naïve, simple Carleton Grines, alias Billmeyer. Evidently, he had a bum ticker ... Don't make any sudden moves now, please, Counsellor, because I'm really very handy with a gun. And when it comes to that fatal tightening of the finger on the trigger, I don't have that momentary qualm which assails so many men at the psychological moment."

Selby, sparring for time, said, "You planned things rather cleverly."

Gillespie smiled. "You're trying to flatter me into giving you incriminating information. However, why not? Once you even suspected me, I was lost. Those damn fingers of mine – and my fingerprints!"

"How long had you known Carleton Grines?" Selby asked.

"Ever since the Oregon jail break. I liked him. He was impetuous and a bit wild, but an attractive, likable chap. Unfortunately, he had married a woman who was all for law and order.

"Now, I had a woman who knew the ropes. Carleton stayed with us for three months, keeping under cover ... Well, there's not much to the rest. She died after about a year. That suit of Carleton's had been carefully saved in a camphorwood chest. Carleton went in the grocery business. He had that peculiar something which makes for business success. Naturally, he became my meal ticket.

"Then his wife showed up. That amnesia business I'd thought up for him stood him in good stead, but he had become greedy. In two months he'd have been declared legally dead. Then the brother would step into oil royalties, running fifty to a hundred thousand a year. I told Carleton he had enough as it was, to let the oil royalties go. He wouldn't do it, rang me up from Las Alidas, filled with a crazy idea. He was going to go and call on his brother who he knew was visiting in Las Alidas, pretend he was still a penniless, down-and-out crook, afraid of the law, and work out an arrangement by which he'd let his brother keep a third of the royalties, provided he passed on the two-thirds. It was crazy.

"That was the call Freelman heard. I was calling Billmeyer in Hollywood and he called me from Las Alidas while I was waiting on the Hollywood call. I told him that real estate deal was ready to close, and that his brother could wait. I got him to promise he'd wait right there until I could get there.

"So I got rid of Freelman and drove over – but first I put some knockout drops in a flask. He'd started drinking again, and I couldn't ever do a thing with him when he'd been drinking. He should have taken a drink and gone to sleep. When he awakened, I could have reasoned with him.

"Well, you know what happened. He went out like a light. When I saw he was dead, I'll confess I was in an awful jam. I left the body in my car, drove over here, ditched the body, went back to Las Alidas, found the place where the brother was staying, and stole Hinkle's car … You know the rest. Under ordinary circumstances, the sheriff would have received my telephone call, started up here, and been in time to see the runaway car careening down the hill. Even if that car hadn't hit anything – and it was almost certain to – the idea would have been the man died of too much drink and a weak heart. The sheriff would have had the man's name – and an Oklahoma check-up would have shown that another drunken carstealer had gone West. In the morning I took the train to Las Alidas, picked up my own car and drove it back.

"And I was thirty-five thousand to the good. Billmeyer had that on him in cash. He'd drawn out a big roll after his wife had called on him, so that if she talked to the police, and he had to get out fast, he'd have enough cash for a stake.

"Well, I haven't any time to waste. By morning I have to be where I can lose myself and not leave any back trail. I'll take you along as hostage, Selby. We'll take my car. You can drive. I'll sit at your side with the gun in my hand – and don't think I won't use it if I have to … Fido, you stay here. Lie down, Fido. *Stay there!* Come on, Selby."

Holding the gun against Selby's back, Gillespie rushed him out to the garage, opened the door, and prodded him in behind the wheel of the big sedan. "You drive. That'll keep your hands occupied. Drive just as I tell you. Don't think you can ditch the car and take a chance on getting away with it, because this revolver is going to be cocked and pressed right against your side. The first jar will pull the trigger. I may survive a wreck, but you won't. Get started."

Selby backed the car out of the garage, headed it down the street.

"Straight ahead," Gillespie said, "and perhaps it's occurring to you, Counsellor, that this is the exact route taken by the death car on Thanksgiving night. I drove it to the top of the hill about ten blocks from my house, then telephoned and waited. If it hadn't been for that neat little bit of detective work you did, I would have got away with my scheme all right. And if it hadn't been for that dog – Oh, well, Selby, that's the way with life. We live and learn. Little things grow into big things. Think of it. I'd just about built up an entirely new personality for myself. Madison City was beginning to regard me as an influential citizen. Well, it was bound to happen sooner or later. Billmeyer was bound to break. When his wife showed up, that really gave him a jolt. I should have known that was the end."

"Shall I stop for that boulevard intersection?" Selby asked.

Gillespie was smiling. "Certainly. Be sure to comply with all the laws, Selby. Be *very* careful about that. I wouldn't want to have some officer stop us for a traffic violation."

Selby raised his eyes to the rear-view mirror. Lights were coming along behind them, lights that were coming fast.

Selby slowed, brought the car to a stop, then purposely clashed the gears in getting started.

Abruptly Selby felt the gun prodding into his side. "Selby, you're damn clever. That's the sheriff's car behind. I hope you haven't been able to signal him some way. Get started. Turn to the right and get going. Remember, Selby, if they try to stop us, that's your death warrant. Go ahead now."

Selby swung the car to the right, conscious that the car behind was swinging in close to them.

Gillespie kept his face forward, his head down. "Don't look back, Selby," he warned. "Start speeding up. When you get it up to fifty, hold it there. You –"

Abruptly the car behind came gliding forward under the swift impetus of speed.

Gillespie's face tightened. "Selby," he said, "I'm afraid you've been too smart for your own good. I hate to do this, but – "

The blood-red spotlight of the county car blazed into brilliance. The sound of the siren knifed the night.

Selby saw Gillespie's lips tighten.

The district attorney slammed on the brake hard, slid the car abruptly to the left, directly in the path of the sheriff's automobile.

The sudden application of the brakes threw Gillespie forward against the windshield. Selby let go the wheel, made a grab for the gun arm, and missed.

Selby heard the roar of the gun, felt a hot stab of flame; then the impact of the sheriff's car.

The cars, with wheels locked, slid and twisted around the wet road in a mêlée of confusion. Selby, his arms flung around Gillespie, groped vainly for the hand that held the gun.

He was vaguely conscious of a white bridge rail ahead, but all his faculties were concentrated on grasping the wrist that held the gun before there could be a second shot.

Just as his fingers touched the wrist, he felt the jar of recoil, heard the gun roar again. But simultaneously with that explosion, a white pole blazed momentarily in front of the headlights, then crashed against Gillespie's automobile. Selby felt his fingers clutch on Gillespie's wrist even as the door flew open and they catapulted out into the darkness.

There was a sensation of falling, a determination on Selby's part to hold firmly to that wrist. Then he was falling – falling ... He struck on a wet bank, skidded downward. Something crashed against his head.

Chapter Eighteen

Selby drifted on that vague borderline between consciousness and the black void of oblivion, now vaguely conscious of events and surroundings, now engulfed by intervals of dark void. Voices ... flashlights ... white-faced, curious spectators. Sylvia holding his head, warm lips on his forehead, the splash of tears against his face ... sirens, red lights ... Harry Perkins' voice, "Here's the ambulance." ... The smell of antiseptics ... Dr Trueman bending over him, the dry, competent voice of the physician, saying, "*That's* not blood. It's lipstick." ... The sting of a hypodermic needle ... a salty taste in his mouth, and the darkness becoming warm, as a cloak of drug-induced slumber was wrapped around him.

Selby awakened late on Sunday morning. A nurse said, "Good morning. How do you feel?"

Selby tried to bring the walls of the room into focus. "I don't know," he said thickly. "How should I feel? Can I see people?"

"Very briefly. Dr Trueman wants me to notify him as soon as you awaken. The sheriff also asked me to call. A Miss Martin has been waiting. She says she's one of the family."

"I want to see Miss Martin," Selby said.

"You'll have to be very brief and you mustn't become excited. Don't ask about news."

Sylvia Martin came in smiling. "Hello, Doug. Guess you're making it okay."

"You knew it was Gillespie?" be asked.

"Uh huh. I beat it for the sheriff's car as soon as I heard the dog bark. Boy, oh boy, did I do some tall sprinting! Listen, Doug, you're not supposed to ask questions. I think Dr Trueman is treating you for a concussion, but I'll just let you peek at something."

She opened her jacket. An extra edition of *The Clarion* was held flat across her chest, so that Selby could read the big headlines:

DA CALLS A TURN

MURDERER, FATALLY WOUNDED, MAKES DEATHBED CONFESSION

Selby tried to reach for the paper. Sylvia Martin drew back, hastily buttoning her jacket. "No, no, Doug. You're not supposed to get excited."

"Would that excite me?" he asked.

"Would it! And listen, the Los Angeles paper certainly gave you a boost. Joe Raft has made a human interest story about the way you outwitted Carr. Doug, don't you feel like jumping up and down in bed and yelling? The whole town's just bursting with pride."

Selby closed his eyes for a moment.

"I remember when Doc Trueman got me to the hospital last night," he said, having some difficulty making the words come clearly, "I heard him say, 'That's not blood. That's lipstick.' But it must have been blood – or was I dreaming?"

Sylvia Martin looked quickly at the door. "Well, as district attorney, I suppose you're entitled to an answer. You see, it was like this," she said, bending swiftly over him.

Erle Stanley Gardner

The Case of the Careless Cupid

Selma Arlington is engaged to a wealthy widower. His heirs don't want him to tie the knot. Perry Mason is asked by Selma to prove she is neither a gold-digger nor a murderer of her first husband, but incriminating evidence comes to light.

The Case of the Fenced-in Woman

Morley Eden finds an unwanted guest on his property. The ex-wife of his dream house's contractor claims that the property is one-half hers. Eden calls upon Perry Mason to resolve a dispute that is linked to murder.

Erle Stanley Gardner

The Case of the Mischievous Doll

A mysterious young woman, Dorrie Ambler, wishes to prove her identity to Perry Mason. She wants him to witness her appendectomy scar, claiming she has a double. The double turns out to be Minerva Minden, madcap heiress of Montrose. Mason has his work cut out for him when his investigation leads him to a dead man in an apartment building.

The Case of the Phantom Fortune

Horace Warren pays five hundred dollars to have Perry Mason attend a buffet dinner to observe his guests. He also wants Mason to investigate a fingerprint and suspects his wife is being blackmailed. Mrs Warren's mystery past may hold the clues.

ERLE STANLEY GARDNER

THE CASE OF THE POSTPONED MURDER

Perry Mason is hired to protect Mae Farr from a presumed stalker, wealthy playboy Penn Wentworth. When Mason learns that Wentworth wants Mae for forging his name on a cheque, things get complicated. But fatal gunplay leaves Wentworth dead, Mae a wanted woman and Perry Mason in trouble.

THE CASE OF THE RESTLESS REDHEAD

Evelyn Bagby has ambition, bad luck – and red hair. When she is caught with stolen diamonds it looks like an airtight case. But Perry Mason believes she has been set up. Then comes news of another crime and Mason finds the charge against his client is murder.